A SPELLBOOKED
MYSTERY

WHAT THE SPELL?

ELLE WREN BURKE

First published by Soaring Moon Books LLC in 2025

Copyright © 2025 by Elle Wren Burke

Print ISBN: 979-8-9990367-0-4

Book cover design by Getcovers.

Chapter One

When I pictured my wedding as a little girl, sobbing and cutting up my wedding dress while still wearing it never made the agenda. Neither did a torrent of fuchsia sparks erupting from my skin, sending the scissors flying across the bridal suite into the wood paneling.

My tears gave way to a yelp when the pink energy exploded my bouquet into a sunset of violet and orange petals, closely followed by the bridesmaid dresses bursting into taffeta confetti. I shut my eyes as an unnatural wind surged through the room. The furniture trembled. Something snapped beneath me. I heard several sharp cracks, and I swear I smelled a faint bit of smoke.

As the room stilled, I opened my eyes to find a half-scorched wedding program floating by, its text declaring Kinley Paigewright would wed Aaron Steel in one hour. I curled my fingers into the sliced-and-diced puff of silk around me—which my handiwork with the scissors had *drastically* improved—as I relived Aaron's declaration that I was too *broken* for him.

My breaths came quickly and a soft glow arose from my skin, but then a shriek tore through the room, startling me out of my spiral. The wedding planner, Shelia, leaned on the door, holding her mangled blue glasses in one hand and clutching her tangled hair with the other.

Oops. I'd forgotten she'd been standing there, trying to convince me to let go of the scissors.

Footsteps sounded in the hall. The door flew open, and Shelia fell into the venue manager's arms. Their squawks of confusion would draw more attention soon. I had to figure out how to contain the situation, but even a public relations account executive—or former account executive, since Aaron had made me quit to run the PR for his state senate campaign—couldn't gloss over the bride turning into an explosive cotton candy machine.

Pushing off the wonky ottoman, I held my hands up...and the two women stiffened.

They didn't simply freeze in fear. Every muscle ceased to move, with Shelia's eyelids raised so I could see the whites all around her irises as she pointed at the stainless-steel light fixture that had found a new home in the middle of a chaise lounge.

I turned my palms over as a flicker of panic tightened my throat. How had I frozen the women? I'd been about to ask them to calm down, and in a way, they had. But would they stay like that forever?

"No, no, no." I flung my fingers out. "Unfreeze!" Nothing happened.

"I did that, not you," a low voice said.

My ankle protested as I twisted around in my silver stilettos to find a white man with blond hair fixing me with an annoyed glare from three feet behind me.

I took a step away, glass crunching under my heel. "Who are you? Where the frick did you come from?" No doors lined the back of the room.

He tapped three shining bronze letters clipped to the chest pocket of his black twill jacket: MBI.

"Umm, okay." I moved my other foot back. This guy had several inches on me with the heels, even more without, and an athletic build, so I needed some distance between us. "I'm just going to take a bathroom break."

He narrowed his caramel eyes. "Oh no, you aren't getting out of this. You've used magic in front of humans. I have to write you a ticket, and you'll need to appear in court. You know the law."

My muscles went stiller than Shelia's. Did he say magic? Magic.

I shook my head. No way. Had pink energy escaped from me? Yes. Did it have a scientific explanation? Also, yes. Spontaneous combustion was real, so why not the spontaneous detonation of one's bridal suite?

The scissors embedded in the wood paneling caught my eye. I strode over and yanked them out of the wall.

"Really? You're going to threaten me with scissors?" the man said. He pinched the bridge of his nose. "Now I have to arrest you."

I flicked my gaze between the scissors and my wedding dress before looking up at the man...who now held a pair of handcuffs in one hand and a tiny black *dragon* in the other.

Well, the dragon confirmed it.

A laugh bubbled up, and within seconds, I was bent over, wiping at the smoky eyeshadow I hadn't wanted to wear.

"Are you okay?" the man asked in the mumbled, dubious tone of someone who knew you were *not* okay.

"This isn't real." I dropped the scissors and twirled, catching sight of myself in the mirror. My long black hair, once curled to perfection, was now as messy as the smear of gray makeup overtaking my green eyes. I looked like a banshee in a shredded designer gown, my pasty white skin enhancing the effect. "All of this is in my head. I'm having a medical incident, likely from emotional turmoil and stress combined with migraines."

He took in my cut-up cupcake of a dress and the remnants of the surrounding decorations. "Oooh." His sharp cheekbones softened a bit. "I take it your wedding is...no longer occurring."

"Yep." Had he not realized that the second he walked into the room? Given that he wasn't real, I supposed I could forgive him.

The man pocketed the cuffs. "That's an understandable reason to have a magical eruption. Did any other humans see, or just the two women by the door?"

With an "oomph," I plopped onto the chaise and rested an arm on the embedded light fixture. "Just those two. Not that it matters. I need to figure out how to wake up. It must be like getting yourself out of a nightmare. Oh! Can you slap me?"

He reared back, and his bright-red sneakers scuffed the floors. "You want me to hit you?"

"Why not?"

"So. Many. Reasons." He slid onto the chaise next to me, keeping as much distance as possible between us. "Look, losing control of your magic in this circumstance is perfectly reasonable. I don't understand why you think this isn't real."

The little dragon in his palm skittered down to his thigh and onto the lounge. I smiled as the creature tilted its head at me. "I've never been one for fantasy books, but this is a fun little addition to my coma. Hi, little one. You're so beautiful."

With a huff of smoke, the dragon puffed its chest out, its scales catching the light.

"You look like your mama dipped you in midnight," I said, holding a finger out.

The man reached out to run the back of his index finger down the dragon's back. "That's his name. Midnight."

I snorted as Midnight nuzzled my knuckle. "Of course, the black dream dragon has the name Midnight. What's your name? Hunky McHunkerson?"

A tinge of red coated his ears, nearly matching his shoes. "I'm sorry?"

"If our names are obvious in this dream, that's yours. Mine's Banshee Bride."

"Right." His lips twitched. "Well, you can call me Detective Fores of the Magical Bureau of Investigation. Only my friends can call me Hunky McHunkerson. And this is not a dream. I need to start modifying the humans' memories."

I snapped my fingers. "See! That right there. You work for the MIB and you change human memories. That's straight out of that movie with Will Smith, you know, *Men in Black*. That proves my dream theory."

Detective Fores ran a hand down the back of his short blond hair. "I work for the M-B-I. The letters are in a different order. We modify human memories with spells, not little devices with red lights."

"Sure, Hunky. Whatever you say. Now, slap me."

He just groaned, so I reached back and whacked my palm into his pale cheek.

"Oww! What the spell?"

I shrugged. "I'm just trying to show you it's okay to slap me since this isn't real."

Rubbing his cheek, he said, "Hexes, I cannot deal with this right now. Hold still." He reached into his jacket and pulled out an ebony wand the length of my forearm. "May I?" He moved the tip of the wand toward my hand.

I jerked away. Dream or not, I didn't want a wand near me. "What are you doing, Detective McHunkerson?"

"Just a gentle test. It won't hurt. Trust me."

My hands crumpled the silk of my gown again as I searched his eyes. After a few seconds, I looked at Midnight. "What do you think?"

The dragon released a chirp with a cloud of steam.

Now that the dream dragon approved, I held my hand out. Detective Fores pressed the wand tip into my palm and uttered a few words under his breath. Cerulean magic hugged me like a warm towel straight out of the dryer. I felt it slide under my skin and settle into my veins, where it mingled with something else, something that felt like falling asleep in your favorite chair with a book on your chest.

My heart fluttered, and a sense of home I hadn't felt in decades settled on my shoulders. The blue magic pulled away, but my magic stayed.

Because I knew now—*my magic* had felt like home, like a cozy nap with a novel on a rainy day.

Detective Fores took a deep breath. "Either you or someone else suppressed your magic until today. I understand your dream theory now, but I assure you, this is real."

"I know." Tapping my heart, I said, "I felt it."

My eyes took in the room. "My magic created quite the chaos." Good. I thought of Aaron's cold eyes when he'd accused me of lying about how bad my migraines had gotten. When he'd sneered at me for embarrassing him at the rehearsal dinner when I'd had to stumble from the room in a dizzy, painful haze. I hoped Aaron and his family had to pay exorbitant damages for my destruction.

But as that feeling of being wrapped in a blanket with a book and a flashlight faded and my eyes moved between the motionless women in the doorway, the dragon on the couch, and the man who'd appeared from nowhere—the man I'd just called hunky and *smacked in the face*—my stomach swirled.

Magic existed.

Magic that could destroy rooms, freeze people, change memories, and who knew what else?

Little black spots overtook my vision.

My throat shrank, head spun, thoughts dragged, shoulders shook.

"What's your name?" Detective Fores's voice sounded far away, but I felt him get on his knees in front of me.

My teeth chattered. It took me two tries to get my name right. "K-Kin—Kinley."

"Are you okay, Kinley? Can you take a deep breath? I'll do it with you."

He took a monstrous breath, big enough for me to follow along.

"Good," he said, and I felt Midnight press his head against my forearm. "What's your last name?"

"P-Pai—Paigewright."

His voice lost its reassuring quality. "Wait, did you say Paigewright?"

"Y-yes."

"Do you have any family here today?"

I shook my head. "No. Family. Ever." It was just me. I didn't even have Aaron anymore. But apparently, I had magic.

With a strangled cry, I hopped onto my heels, almost knocking Detective Fores over, and started to pace.

Alone. So alone. Magic. So much magic.

As my thoughts swirled, so did my magic, as if I could spin panic into magic like Rumpelstiltskin could spin straw into gold. Slivers of fuchsia leaked from my skin until a pulsing aura surrounded me.

Detective Fores paced alongside me. "Kinley! Calm down. Just breathe."

"Can't." I stared at the now-sparking magic. "No, no, no!" I choked on the thick magic in my throat. It built until every cell had surely saturated with pink energy. We had seconds. "Help!"

I turned desperate eyes on Detective Fores only to be met with the swish of his jacket as he wrapped himself around me and threw us both down, straight into a gaping black hole in the ground that sealed behind us with a snap.

Chapter Two

A cloud of pink magic, like a thousand cherry blossoms, burst from me when I realized we floated in an endless night sky devoid of stars. The energy cascaded from my skin in all directions, and I braced for impact, but before my magic could send my stilettos sailing, the magic imploded, shrinking into a random point in space until every spark had receded into nothing.

Where had Detective Fores taken me? Some kind of magic-eating no man's land? Would he leave me here so I couldn't hurt anyone else?

But then another hole opened below us, and we tumbled down. With his arms still around me, he rolled us to take the impact on his back, and I landed on his chest.

The sun revealed gold stipples in his eyes as I narrowed my own to scowl at him. "I was going to apologize for hitting you earlier, but now that you dragged me through the space-time continuum without consent, I think I'll pass." A chirp from his pocket made me smile. "Midnight agrees." Thank goodness the little guy survived our fall.

"Fair enough, but do you think you could..." Detective Fores waved his hand.

"Oh, right." I rolled off him and precariously pushed to my feet, taking care not to sprain an ankle. Why had I ever agreed to wear these awful heels? "So, what was that place?" I looked up, expecting to see the parking lot of Portland's premier wedding venue. "Some kind of black hole or—" My words died, eaten like the black hole that had consumed my magic.

I stood on a wide brick sidewalk flanking a long street lined with two- and three-story buildings. My eyes flipped from business to business, catching names like Witch Stitch, Fairy Tale Treasures, and The Unicorn's Uncle. People gave us a wide berth as they moved down the street, and I couldn't blame them, given the whole banshee bride situation. Detective Fores stood and extracted Midnight, who shook out his leathery wings before clinging to the detective's shoulder.

"Where are we?" I asked, watching a kid blow bubbles made of rich chocolate.

He set a comforting hand on my shoulder. "I had to take you to Portland's closest magical town, which is where I live and work. The Sea Sprite branch oversees any magical irregularities in Oregon and—"

"Ryland, honey. It looks like you're having quite the day."

We both turned to find a smiling East Asian woman with graying black hair cut sharply at her collarbone step from the shop behind us. She crossed the bricks in her sensible walking shoes to pull Detective Fores—Ryland—into a hug.

Ryland gave her a tight squeeze before he directed her attention to me. "My day has proved interesting, but Kinley's having a spell of a day."

The corners of the woman's eyes crinkled. "I can see that." She extended a hand, her bronze skin shining in the late afternoon light. "Sylvie Choi."

"Kinley Paigewright," I said as we shook.

Sylvie's firm grip loosened as I spoke my last name. Her eyes flicked to a shop, not the one she'd left, but the one beside it. The Perfect Page. With a raised brow, she turned to Ryland.

He gave her a tight nod. "Kinley just learned about magic today. After her wedding...ah...failed to occur. I need to go modify some memories and repair extensive damage. Can you explain...everything?"

"Of course. Go!"

Wait, Ryland was leaving me here? I knew nothing about this place. But before I could protest, he opened another doorway of darkness and stepped through, Midnight blending into the nothingness.

"Portal magic," Sylvie said, twirling an earbud that dangled on a cord around her neck. "Ryland has a fairly rare ability to open rifts in space at will. It's part of what makes him a great asset to the MBI. Now, would you like to come inside my shop?" She pointed to the storefront she'd emerged from a minute before. A wall of windows sat below a plum-purple awning that read Pegasus Potions with a white-winged horse soaring over the silver script.

Potions. Potions that could do *anything* to me.

Poison me. Turn me into a toad. Color my toenails electric blue forever.

I felt uncontrolled magic rising for the third time that day. "Where are we? Why am I here?"

"This is Sea Sprite Isle, and your new home—"

"WHAT?" My bare arms glowed. I took a step back and bumped into someone. I turned to apologize but lost all ability to speak as I stared at the tall woman's glossy, viridian wings. She gave me a confused look, so I tore my eyes away only for them to land on a teenager turning into a fox.

I slid my fingernails into my palms and forced a breath. Witches, dragons, and now a winged woman and a fox shifter. This was fine. I was fine.

Then the cry of a gull above reminded me that Sylvie had declared this to be an *island* and *my new home*. I looked up to watch the gull soar past and spotted a man on a broomstick swooping in time with the bird.

Not fine. At all. Nausea snaked up my throat. I twisted until I found a group of gulls in the distance, and I took off in their direction. Sylvie called after me, but I ignored her.

Cursing my heels the whole way, I ran past a man floating three huge boxes with a wand, two more winged women with pointed ears who launched into the air, a pedicab propelling itself down the street, and hundreds of other magical beings and objects I couldn't process.

The road curved and shifted into colorful residences, the sidewalk narrowing and growing less crowded. Crashing waves announced the ocean before I saw it, my gut sloshing with each resounding swell.

When I rounded the last bend, I stopped with the tips of my satin shoes a centimeter from the rocky sand. Mist hugged the shore, but through a gap, I could see a stretch of land in the distance.

A few small boats had been tied to a dock nearby, but even if I were up for grand theft boat, I didn't have the skills to make it across that wide span of water.

I sank down, letting the now-uneven hem of my dress hit the sand. Ryland had trapped me here. The fuchsia shine faded back into my skin as panic gave way to hopelessness. A chill set in, my body realizing that I wore a strapless gown at the beach in September.

No fiancé. No job. I could handle that. I'd been there before. But I thought I was done being forced into homes. I thought I'd gained my independence the moment I'd turned eighteen and left the foster system.

A soft sound pulled my gaze from the cresting waves to the witch climbing off a transparent broom handle filled with a sloshing, iridescent periwinkle liquid—like a potion. Sylvie sat, her knees creaking, and rested the broom on her dark jeans, the velvety lavender bristles brushing against her fitted purple T-shirt and long gray cardigan.

"Kinley, I'm sorry. I worded that poorly. Scaring you wasn't my intention. You don't need to fear anything on Sea Sprite Isle."

I scoffed.

She patted my goosebump-covered arm. "Let me explain. From what Ryland said, I assume your magic detonated from you, causing some property damage? And from how you two landed on the ground when you got to town, I'm guessing you had another burst brewing when Ry opened the portal?"

"Yes. I exploded inside the portal."

"Ryland grabbed you just in time then," she said, her affection for the detective clear in her voice. "Given how new you are to magic, it's safer for you and humans if you stay here. That being said, we wouldn't imprison you here, Kinley. You have to learn to control your magic. We can help you on the island, or you can figure something out at home. I hope you might choose to stay, though, because, well...Sea Sprite Isle was once your home."

I leaned away from her. "Umm...no. Someone left me at a fire station only a few days after my birth. You have me confused with someone else." I patted my knees. "So, who else around here can do portal magic? And maybe someone can just lock down my magic again before I return to Portland? That will solve the problem. I've got to talk to my old boss and get my job back." My mind started spinning on all the ways I could salvage my career, starting with how to explain things to my boss.

Unbidden, a press release took shape in my mind, as they so often did:

Mr. Aaron Steel has decided to not-at-all amicably end his engagement to Miss Kinley Paigewright just one-hour prior to their ceremony by being a human barnacle worthy only of growing inside a portable toilet next to the spiciest food truck at a multi-day music festival. Mr. Steel has accused her of lying about her migraines, which is just so mean and uncalled for, especially because he simply wasn't paying attention when she told him in detail about her medical situation. Furthermore, Mr. Steel was apparently only using Miss Paigewright for her "rags-to-riches or-phan story" and her PR skills, both of which he thought would help his political campaigns. Therefore, no one should blame Miss Paigewright for pulling magic out of her butt to blow up the ridiculously expensive wedding venue at which his controlling family insisted the couple wed.

"Kinley?"

I looked at Sylvie. Oops. "Sorry, did you say something?"

"Yes, I said that no one here would suppress your magic, dear. And..." She bit her lip. "Kinley, tell me what you know about your last name."

"Whoever abandoned me left it on a note tucked into my blanket. My name is the only thing I know about myself, but the authorities couldn't link anyone to me. I looked when I got old enough, but I couldn't find anyone either."

Sylvie swiveled on the pavement and grabbed my hands. "That's because your family lives in the magical world. We couldn't find *you* either. I think that piece of paper with your name must have held a spell. As soon as the humans read the words, the spell hid you from us. Kinley, we looked. Your mother...she left Sea Sprite at nine months pregnant and only twenty-two years old. She took your father and told no one else. She never returned. I can't believe you've lived just a couple hours away in Portland all this time."

One blink. Two. Three. My mind couldn't do anything except raise and lower my eyelids. I gently pulled away from Sylvie's hands and dropped my head into what remained of my voluminous gown. "Okay," I said, voice muffled by beaded silk. "Am I seriously sitting on a brisk beach in a shredded wedding dress with a *fellow witch* and finally, finally, after over thirty-two years, learning about my birth family?"

Sylvie's voice dropped to just above a whisper. "I'm afraid so, but there's so much more."

Pressure built behind my left eye and my temples throbbed. I groaned.

Sylvie pushed to her feet. "C'mon. Let's go to my shop. You're freezing. I'll get you a warm drink and something to eat, then I'll tell you everything I know."

Chapter Three

The slow walk back—because no way in *spell* was I getting on the back of Sylvie's frickin' broomstick—gave me time to see what I'd missed during my frantic dash.

A purple street sign told me we ambled down Trouble Avenue, where we passed Merlin's Magic Supply, Wishing Well Wines, and The Moon Bear's Oven. When the door opened to the latter, I almost fainted when my nose caught the spiced potatoes folded into a samosa held by an exiting customer. I could have snatched it out of his greedy hands.

Forcing my eyes back to the street, I looked at Clay & Cauldron, a magical pottery studio, and Spellbound, a custom spell shop.

Sylvie chuckled at my wide-eyed wonderment. "We have a parallel street called Toil and several bisecting streets named after other lines in Shakespeare's famous scene."

Ah, from *Macbeth*. "'Double, double toil and trouble,'" I recited. "'Fire burn and cauldron bubble.'"

"Exactly. We're coming up on Double, Double Street, right after Wicked Witch Wands."

I paused in front of the picture windows displaying the wand shop's name in curling sapphire letters. The glare from the late-afternoon sun aggravated my brewing migraine, but I shoved the pain down. "Will I get a wand?"

Sylvie stopped beside me. "Yes, honey. You can choose any wand or wands you'd like."

My eyes roved over the bright display case, taking in a long emerald wand with an amethyst set into a black handle, a short white wand with two cores twisted like DNA, and a black wand with a blue button. A sign next to it marked it as collapsible.

That seemed quite practical. Considering a strapless gown had become my sole piece of clothing, where would I store a long piece of wood? Sign me up for collapsible.

I dropped my gaze to the bottom shelf, and it locked onto a slender wand with a violet handle and a shaft wrapped in creamy paper printed in dark, typewritten ink.

"Sylvie, that wand has book pages on it!"

I wanted to rush into the store to purchase it, whether it collapsed or not, but I didn't have my wallet. If I thought the owner would have traded for a destroyed designer gown, I'd have stripped right there in the street.

Books had always been my savior. Growing up in foster care had started off easy and comfortable for me, but by age nine, things had changed drastically, and I'd entered a revolving door of homes with only one constant: books.

Sylvie took my arm. "Let's get you a bit more settled before arming you with a wand, okay? Though, I must say, I'm glad you like that particular wand. It bodes well for our conversation."

That sparked my interest, so I let her lead me back to Pegasus Potions as fast as my heels would allow—slower than a cursed crone. My stilettos had protested my earlier sprint by rubbing my skin raw.

The sounds around us seemed to build as we walked, but I knew my migraine played tricks on me. I rubbed at my temples and narrowed my eyes a bit to shield my pupils from the light.

When a bell tinkled upon our entry to Pegasus Potions, rich cinnamon and nutmeg mixed with a bit of citrus swept up my nose. A curly-haired white woman with a Pegasus Potions apron over her soft curves worked behind a long weathered-walnut counter, ringing up a man's many purchases. A wall of copper, silver, and gold bottles and vials with ivory labels towered behind her. Their opaqueness stood in stark contrast to the products on the shop floor.

Shelves and tables overflowing with transparent bottles, vials, and jars full of colorful liquids and salves blossomed around me. I ran my finger over the grain of the closest table, the wood an exact match for the sales counter. My nail grazed over a sign for a ten-second pimple cream, and my inner teenager's jaw dropped.

Sylvie bustled around, waving at perusing customers and grabbing items with her broomstick tucked under her arm. Meanwhile, I discovered a rainbow hair potion—one color every four hours, rotating over four days; a solution to restore your wood floors to their original, gleaming state; and a potion to make you sing beautifully for four hours.

"Kinley, back here."

The wood floors—also walnut—creaked as I followed Sylvie past another employee helping a talkative woman and through a wide doorway behind the register. We passed through a storeroom to a comfortable employee lounge with pale blue walls, a gray settee, and a black table with four chairs.

While I plopped on the settee in a plume of chopped silk, Sylvie leaned her broom against the wall and set a bottle, a vial, and a jar on a small counter. She uncorked the electric-blue vial and held it out to me.

I shrank back, clutching at the linen armrest beside me. "What is it?"

"This potion heals headaches, and you clearly have one." When I didn't accept, she poured a small measure into a mug on the counter and drank it. "See? Not poisonous."

My left eye ached as I stared at the potion, the overhead fluorescent lights beating down on my brain. "Screw it. After the day I've had, I might as well swallow my first potion too."

I took the cool glass and tossed back the pepper-mint-flavored liquid. I waited with closed eyes for either death or relief, and after a minute, the latter found me. Lifting my eyelids, I discovered the light still bothered me, but not nearly as much. The pain in my eye had receded to a small pulse, and the pounding in my temples had ceased. "Thank you, Sylvie. That didn't stop my migraine, but it helped."

She tucked a strand of graying hair behind her ear and beamed at me. "Good. Potions to turn your grass pink for a month make me laugh, but healing potions are why I do this. Now..." Sylvie turned to grab the small jar, opening it with a pop that would have rattled my head moments ago. "Put this on your feet."

I happily accepted the salve, rubbing the thick paste into my cuts. The wounds sealed in just three heartbeats, and I looked at Sylvie with my jaw practically underneath the floorboards.

She laughed, the sound filling the small room. "You'll see much more impressive things, Kinley." Sylvie handed me the third product, along with some cotton balls. "Makeup remover."

I scrubbed at my face until she confirmed I'd cleaned it all. I tended toward a bit of mascara and lip balm, so the whole bride-who-might-be-about-to-murder-you look was not for me.

Sylvie took a seat at the table. "Kinley, like I said, we looked for you. We used magical and nonmagical means of searching for your mother, father, and you, but we found nothing. We haven't heard a peep from your parents since they left Sea Sprite Isle."

My stomach clenched. I'd always assumed my parents hadn't wanted me, but what if... "Do you think something happened to them?"

She pulled her lip between her teeth and looked at the table. "We don't know. They had no reason to leave town. It was out of character. Your parents both had a strong sense of responsibility and love for their family. It never made sense. So, it's possible they meant to return but couldn't."

I didn't need magic to discern the subtext. She believed they'd died. A pang tore from my navel to my heart, which seemed ridiculous, given that I'd never known my parents and never expected to know anything about them. I took a deep breath.

"We tried using seers," Sylvie continued, "but we only learned one thing. That you had been separated from your parents. No other details. We couldn't find you. I'm so sorry."

With my mouth suddenly dry, I said, "You aren't to blame. But who else helped search? You keep saying 'we.'"

She crossed her legs. "Your recently deceased grandmother."

"Oh."

Recently.

How close had I come to meeting her? I tugged on a piece of silk until it tore away from the marshmallow I wore.

Sylvie ran her thumbs over the edges of her fingernails. "I can't imagine what it must feel like to finally learn you had family, but that you missed them by just a couple months."

Months. My fingers wiped at my eyes, coming away clean thanks to the makeup remover. "It feels like a wrecking ball to the soul. I lost two families today. Getting married meant I'd officially no longer be alone. I'd have an actual family. Then, after Aaron's sisters didn't show up to get into their bridesmaid dresses, he strolled in wearing a sweater, not a tux. He stood there, looming over me while I sat on an ottoman, telling me I'd misled him about my migraines, embarrassed him by getting dizzy and off-balance at the rehearsal dinner. He said I was too broken. That someone like me couldn't lead his state senate campaign, couldn't be around donors, couldn't be his wife as he made his way to the top. That I'd just make a fool of him. I knew appearances were important to him, but I...I didn't know he cared *this* much. Didn't know *I* meant so little. Now, I find out I had family here, in this magical town, but they're gone."

Sylvie stood and took my hands. "Your grandmother might be gone, but she was my best friend and like a sister. She was my chosen family, Kinley. *I* am your family. You don't know me, but I promise, I'm here for you. Always. You have a home here in Sea Sprite." She reached up to swipe the soft pad of her thumb across my tear-laden cheek. "Aaron sounds like a cockroach, and if you want me to curse him, I've already got four options in mind."

I laughed, a salty tear falling onto my tongue. "Thank you, Sylvie." My heart swelled at the genuine shine in her eyes. I wanted to believe she considered me family, but after Aaron, I felt my drawbridge rising and my moat filling with water.

"She's right," said a low voice from the door by the far wall. I jumped in my seat, but my butt had a built in crash pad with this gigantic dress. "You do have a home here. Literally. And a business." Ryland crossed to the table and set down a familiar black tote bag. "She's right about Aaron too, though cockroach might be too generous a word for him." Midnight emerged from Ryland's pocket and meeped his agreement. The little dragon jumped onto the table.

My lips parted. How long had Ryland stood in the doorway? Had he heard everything I'd said? My pale, traitorous cheeks reddened. I extracted my hands from Sylvie and performed the world's most unnecessary smoothing of a dress. "You brought my bag," I said as Ryland unzipped his jacket and neatly folded it.

"After I fixed the room and modified memories, your wedding planner gathered your things."

As Sylvie and Ryland sat at the table, I stood and grabbed my black tote, dumping a planner, water bottle, wallet, e-reader, and two books onto the table in my search for my special migraine glasses. Midnight sniffed each item. When I found the tan case, I cracked it and slipped on the thick black frames with pink lenses.

"Aaaah." I fell back onto the settee. The last bit of the light sensitivity fizzled away. "So, Aaron won't have to explain away my explosion by saying I recruited a frat house and pumped them full of sugar sticks and Red Bull, then gave them free rein to wreak havoc?"

Ryland's left eyebrow rose just a bit, the movement making me realize his left ear sat a little lower than his right ear. "Umm, no."

"Do you know what happened to the guests?" I asked.

He lifted an ankle onto the opposite knee, displaying those fire engine sneakers. "Some snobby lady in white told the guests the wedding 'would no longer proceed.'" He said the last four words in an impressive impression of a Victorian-era lady.

"Eggshell," I corrected. "Cynthia—Aaron's mother—bought an eggshell dress, not white. She told me she obviously wasn't the bride anyway, so—" I stopped talking when I caught the look Sylvie and Ryland shared. "Oh, who am I kidding? That dress is frickin' white, and Cynthia sucks." I gestured to the bird's butt of a dress I wore. "She chose this." I lifted my feet, extending my legs. "These too, and everything else."

I'd put up with it because I thought Aaron loved me. Satisfying his mother had seemed easier than fighting, and I hadn't given one owl's hoot about which precise shade of purple for the napkin rings would bring out the wood grain in the venue's antique floorboards.

Sylvie got up to fill the kettle. "I'm glad to hear you didn't choose that dress, because now I don't have to brew a potion to cure hideous taste."

I snorted. "You can brew away, and we'll sneak some into Cynthia's nightcap."

Ryland ran a finger over Midnight's tail. "I know you're joking, but I feel compelled to tell you that's illegal."

"Speaking of, don't you need to write me a ticket?"

With a basket of pastries in hand, Sylvie spun around. "Don't you dare, Ryland Fores."

He held his hands up. "Don't worry. Your case falls into a legal gray area. Given the situation, my ticket pad will stay in my jacket. Unless you decide to slip a human a potion." He wrinkled his nose as he looked at my dress, and my stomach gave a curious stir, like a little dragon tail had sloshed the contents around. "Even if that potion would do the world a favor. You really did improve that dress by taking scissors to it."

Sylvie chuckled as she handed me a mug of tea and a flower-shaped pastry. "Maybe spill some tea on the dress too. And eat this; it's a Korean red bean bun."

I chomped happily on the soft and sweet bun. No matter how hard Aaron had pushed, I'd never given up carbs. Baked goods gave me the courage to wake up in the morning.

I took a sip of tea, making sure to slosh some onto the dress.

Halfway through the bun, I almost dropped it on the floor when a raccoon strolled into the room on two legs.

Midnight chirped a few times, but the humans didn't react as it climbed onto the table.

"Umm, can you two see the raccoon, or do I have some kind of witchy ability to see animal ghosts?"

The raccoon curled its long body around the tiny dragon.

"Oh!" Sylvie ran a hand down the raccoon's back. "This is my familiar, Dusk." The gray critter raised its head to assess me. "She says you smell like humans and an abundance of cortisol, which makes sense, given your stressful day. Dusk would also like you to know that your grandmother was her second favorite human."

I stared. "She...talks."

"Only to me, just as Midnight speaks only to Ryland."

Midnight gazed at Ryland with adoring eyes, and the detective stroked the dragon's chin with his finger. "Midnight really likes you, Kinley." Ryland flicked his eyes to mine. "He usually takes more time to appreciate someone, but he took to you right away."

My chest warmed like the little guy had blown his smoke right into my heart. "What a sweetheart. I like you too, Midnight."

We watched the familiars snuggle as I finished my pastry. "So, I have my wallet now. Can I find somewhere to sleep?" Now that I knew they wouldn't force me to stay here, I figured I should learn to control my magic before returning to Portland, so hopefully Sea Sprite had a comfortable inn.

Ryland uncrossed his legs. "I meant what I said earlier. You literally have a home here. Your grandmother left everything to her grandchild, if we ever located them, so you own her house and business."

A house? I had a one-bedroom condo back in Portland. I didn't need an entire house for just me. But I was curious about it. The system had bounced me from place to place over the years, and I knew you could learn a lot about someone the second you walked into their living space. What would this house tell me about my grandmother?

"What kind of business did she own?" I could always sell it and the house and invest the money in my own PR firm once I left the island.

Sylvie twirled her earbuds. "A bookshop. It's next door."

"Oh! I saw it. The Perfect Page. Cute name."

Ryland's lips quirked. "It's also an accurate name. The shop knows what book each customer needs. Though, of course, everyone is welcome to browse for whatever they want."

Okay, that was cool. "So, someone put a spell on the shop?" That should boost the sale price.

"Not exactly," Sylvie said, eyes flitting to the ceiling.

"Some other kind of magic, then?"

She swiped her teeth over her lip. "Yes, it's called bibliomancy. Only a small percentage of witches have bibliomancy."

"Book magic! That's amazing. I love reading. How cool that a book witch could create a store that always knows just what book to get you."

"Well," Ryland said. "That's true, but..."

Sylvie and Ryland exchanged a cryptic look. These two clearly knew each other well, and could say a lot with a look. I'd have found their friendship adorable, but I wished they'd just spit out whatever they needed to say. "What?"

"The store can't survive on its own," Sylvie finally said. "It must maintain a bond with a bibliowitch at all times or the store dies."

I gulped. "So when my grandmother died, the store died?"

Ryland shook his head. "Not yet, but the process has begun. If a bibliowitch doesn't bond soon, death will come for Page."

"You mean death will come for the magic, right? Why do you keep talking about the store like it's a person?"

Sylvie stood. "Because Page is sentient, Kinley. A sentient shop. And it's time you meet him. Let's go."

Chapter Four

When we stepped onto the brick sidewalk hugging Trouble Avenue, wind whipped my hair around my face. Maybe I needed to shave my head and start over after the havoc the day had wreaked on my mane. I pulled Sylvie's spare cardigan—black and dusted with raccoon fur—closer. My companions led me next door to The Perfect Page, though I found myself tempted to run to the next shop over, Mystic Mugs, which promised coffee and pastries.

I stopped to run my eyes over The Perfect Page's storefront, but other than the magenta awning with a quill-and-ink-pot logo, I couldn't see much. Tall picture windows lined the long space, but despite the peach rays of the afternoon sun hitting them from our right, my eyes couldn't spot even a single book.

Before I could ask Sylvie if magic had darkened the windows, Ryland said from beside me, "Are you doing okay?"

I took a breath of fresh sea air. "Honestly, I have no idea. I feel like I'm in a fever dream, but as we established back at the wedding venue, this is real." Biting my lip, I shifted on my no-longer-aching feet. "I want to apologize."

He bumped his shoulder into mine. "I thought you weren't going to apologize for hitting me after I dragged you through the space-time continuum."

"Oh, I'm not. I'll admit to feeling regret for that, but I want to apologize for...objectifying you while I thought I was dreaming."

Sylvie stepped around me so she faced us both. "Oh, I need to hear this."

One side of Ryland's lips rose. "I can forgive you if you remind me exactly what you said."

"Seriously?"

He crossed his arms, holding firm.

I pinched my brows together. "Fine, I'm sorry I called you," I dropped my voice to a whispered mumble, "*Hunky McHunkerson*."

"What?" Sylvie cupped her ear, a massive grin on her face. "I didn't hear you."

I huffed. "Sorry for calling you Hunky McHunkerson!" My face went pinker than my migraine glasses and dropped to scarlet when a group of passing teenagers giggled.

"I accept your apology," Ryland said, inclining his head.

"If you're going to arrest this harlot, Detective Fores, can you make it quick? She's driving away business."

My neck snapped up, following the loud voice calling to us from the third floor above. A petite wisp of a white woman with limp brown hair leaned over an iron railing painted the exact shade of magenta as the bookshop's awning. I followed the balcony to a set of stairs—also magenta—that led down to the street.

The woman tapped the railing, her floral dress from at least two decades ago rippling in the breeze. "Well? Are you putting her in a cell or what?" She pushed her wire-rim glasses up her nose.

"No," Ryland said. "This is Margaret Paigewright's granddaughter, and this has nothing to do with you, Denise."

Her vertebrae snapped up, one by one. "This harlot is Margaret's granddaughter?" She sneered and thumped her chest. "Then this has everything to do with me."

"Denise," Sylvie said, the warning clear in her voice. She moved to my side again, placing a hand on my arm. "This is not the time."

Aaron had called me a lot of things that morning, and in my shock, I'd let him, but I would not tolerate being called a harlot. Twice. Rage uncoiled in my gut. I. Was. Done.

"Excuse me, lady!" I shouted. "I don't know who you are, but that's an extremely offensive word. Apologize! Now."

Denise gestured down her body. "Look at you. High heels. Some distressed little number like a wannabe Madonna."

She thought my cut-up wedding gown looked like something Madonna would wear? Wow, just wow.

"What else would you be doing in an outfit like that if not acting like a harlot?" she taunted.

"Watch it!" Sylvie scolded as Ryland muttered, "Conjured cosmos, this day is going to kill me."

I barely heard them through the fury narrowing my focus to the woman above, who I had half a mind to chuck a heel at, but my aim sucked, so I said, "Listen, *Denise*, I cut up this wedding gown, and if you don't back off, I'll come up there and cut the shoulder pads out of the 1990s travesty you're wearing."

She let out the fakest gasp I'd ever heard. "You would threaten your tenant?"

I swiveled to Sylvie, the bottom of my cardigan smacking into Ryland. "My what?"

"You own the entire building. There's a commercial space on the third floor. Denise has a lease for another six months, I believe."

"Six months?" I squeaked. If I stayed, I'd have to deal with this, well, witch. And if I left Sea Sprite, would anyone buy the shop if it came with Denise's lease?

"That's right," my nasty tenant called down. "Six months. And we have things to discuss."

Ryland lifted his arms. "Take a breath, Denise. You have plenty of time to review any grievances at a later date. In private." His voice rung with authority, but I pushed in front of him.

I put my hands on the hips of my apparently salacious dress. "No, I'd like to know what's so important she has to yell it down three floors my first day on this island!"

Denise gave Ryland a satisfied look before asking, "Do you plan to keep selling journals like your harpy grand-mother?"

"Do I..." I gaped at her. "Journals? You want to talk about frickin' *diaries*?"

"Oh my cauldrons, I can't wait to post these two un-hinged old ladies on Hijinx," a squeaky voice said.

"I'm in my early thirties!" I called over my shoulder, unwilling to be called yet another incorrect thing today.

"Yeah, so old," I heard the teenager say.

"Your grandmother insisted on competing with my business." Denise pointed to the sign above her, but I couldn't read it at this angle. "That violates my tenant rights."

Ryland sighed. "It does no such thing."

I moved a few paces back, finally becoming aware of the crowd behind us, but I laughed as I saw the sign. Denise's Stationery. "You opened a stationery store above a bookshop, and you're complaining that the bookshop sells journals?" I crossed my arms. "At least people still buy journals. Who buys stationery these days? I think *email* is your real competitor. Maybe you should be yelling at the email fairies in the street!"

A chorus of mutters broke out behind me, and Ryland leaned down. "Umm, I guess Sylvie didn't tell you, but the winged beings walking around town are fairies."

Oof. Sea Sprite might just kick me out after this interaction. "Sorry!" I called to the crowd. "The magical world is new to me as of today. I'm still learning. I'll do better."

Denise looked pleased as poisoned punch. "You're making quite the impression, Miss Paigewright. Offending local business owners *and* our fairy population."

"Oh, get hexed!" I looked at Sylvie. "Do people say that here?" She nodded.

I could really get on board with magical lingo.

Denise kept talking like she was two stories up on a stage of her own. "You're just as arrogant as Margaret. Maybe more so. When she *finally* died, I had high hopes for someone who would respect their tenant, someone with integrity—"

My body shook so hard my glasses slipped down my nose. "NO!" I bellowed. I may never have met Margaret, but I wasn't about to let this woman portray some venomous version of my grandmother. "One more word, and I'll come up there to stuff a journal down your throat! Then after you choke, I'll pull it out and sell it in my store!"

That made *Ryland* choke, and it grew into a groan as Denise pulled a stubby blue wand out. "I'd like to see you try."

A force I couldn't see sprung to life above me, pulsing with magic. "Put it away, Denise." Ryland's voice carried through the magic, ringing louder than seemed natural.

To my surprise, Denise listened. I turned my head to see the detective's wand out and his face set with unblinking determination.

"Let's go," he said, leading me with a firm but gentle grip on my bicep to the now unlocked door to The Perfect Page. Sylvie stood just inside holding an old-fashioned skeleton key. She shut the door behind us, and the room darkened.

Ryland slowly released my arm. "Just a kernel of advice, Kinley. Maybe don't threaten to kill people in front of MBI detectives." The words were serious, but I could sense the smile behind them.

"I didn't threaten to kill her," I said, turning to face the shop's interior. "I threatened to choke her a little—"

But I choked on the words as I tried to comprehend what awaited me inside the bookshop.

Chapter Five

A wasteland of books surrounded us. Even in the low light, I could tell something *off* permeated this space, something that had leached color from the floors, the furniture, the books.

It had become a literary graveyard, seeped of that warm potential that settled into your chest as you stepped into a bookstore. The spark of a thousand new worlds awaiting you.

Only a dull, gray impression of a bookstore remained. "What happened?" I whispered.

Sylvie spoke even softer. "Like we said, Page is dying."

I gripped the cardigan's collar. "But the books." I looked down at the plush rug under our feet, an intricate pattern of books and vines just visible. "The décor."

"Everything you see *belongs* to Page, became a *part of* Page."

Everything? I swept my eyes over the deep stacks of books, the cozy reading nooks, the staircase to a second floor rimmed by a balcony, behind which sat even more desolate books. How could all this die?

Ryland approached a circular, wooden display table to my left. Ran his finger over the smooth grain. "My mom brought me and my siblings here once a week, but sometimes she'd sneak just me off for a second visit." He smiled and nodded toward an alcove with two squashy armchairs in the corner near the front window. "The chairs would swallow me. I'd tuck all my limbs in and read human-world fantasy books. My mom would read the book along with me as she stood over my shoulder so we could talk about it on the walk home."

Something twisted under my ribs as I looked at that alcove, so bleak now. I could see a little Ryland squeezed into the chair, eyes locked onto the page in front of him. Now, that chair looked like it would turn to dust with a single breath.

Your instincts are correct. It will turn to dust. Everything within my walls will crumble.

I jumped and stumbled, Ryland catching me. I'd handled a lot today, but voices in my head? Nope. Especially not a resounding bass that filled every hollow space in my body.

"Okay, that's enough. Take me back to the human world, I can't handle—"

Don't be afraid, that voice said again. I clutched at my bodice.

"Ah," Sylvie said. "Page is talking to you."

Ryland steadied me and let go. "It's okay, Kinley. You're safe."

He's right. You have never been safer than you are within these walls. With each word, Page's voice deepened and took root, expanding like an oak tree until the branches tickled every corner of my mind.

Page laughed. *That's an apt comparison, considering I'm born of books, and thus, of trees.*

My jaw hung open. This sentient bookshop could read my mind.

Oh, it's more than that. I can read your soul. *I can read everyone's soul, though. It is how I know which book everyone needs, but you are the only mind I can read, since you are a Paigewright bibliowitch. I'm so glad you are here at last.*

The store creaked around me, and it almost felt like Page had taken a breath.

You do not want to bond with me, though, Page said.

"I'm overwhelmed. This is the most overwhelming day of my life."

You do not have to speak to me aloud, unless you want Sylvie and Ryland to hear.

No, I thought, *I don't. They've seen me humiliated enough today.*

Page hummed, a sound like rustling paper. *I wouldn't worry about that, but I understand. Perhaps you should take a seat. I promise, the chair won't wither beneath you. Yet.*

The last word echoed in my head as I crossed to the alcove by the window. I lifted the bundle of toilet paper currently serving as my dress and plunked down.

That gown is hideous, Page said.

I laughed, the sound carrying around the dying room. *Yep. I hate it.*

Good. We haven't had a Paigewright with such bad taste in a century.

I bit the inside of my cheek. How many of my ancestors had Page known? My mother, grandmother, and so many more, while I'd known exactly zero?

Come now, Page said, voice lilting. *I know things have been tough, Kinley, and I know you're upset you missed meeting Margaret and your mother, but you have me now. I am your family.*

Just like Sylvie had said.

Yes, Sylvie and Margaret considered each other family, but we are kin. *Paigewright magic gave me life, birthed me. I have been a part of this family since the 19th century.*

I swallowed. Actual family. I had actual family. A part of me wanted desperately to believe it, but a louder voice told me I'd never have that.

Clutching at the drab chair's arms, I told Page, *You could have a glitch. You could think I'm your family, but I'm just a random witch.*

Page let out a little huff. *I can only communicate with family. Look down.*

I dropped my eyes and sucked in a breath. Beneath my hands, a rich green, not quite emerald, threaded itself through the fibers of the chair. The hue continued to knit itself through every part of the chair I contacted. I pushed my dress aside to watch a book cover come to life on the cushion below me, though I couldn't see the title. Even the floorboards touching my shoes came to life with a cherry stain.

See? Just your presence has restored a kernel of life to me. I won't push you to bond, but... Page trailed off, sounding uncertain for the first time. *Will you consider it?*

I ran my teeth over my bottom lip. *What would it feel like?*

On a daily basis, much like this, but you'd have a stronger read on my emotions, though not to the degree I can read yours. You'd be able to feel the shop, the books, everything. Our connection would also enhance your magic.

My back stiffened. I'd already blown up a bridal suite. Did I really want stronger magic?

What you did to that room today was quite tame. The detective once destroyed an entire classroom at the elementary school because the other children tried to make him hold the class rabbit.

A laugh burst from me, and the entire alcove filled with color, the lamp above me flickering on. I looked at Ryland. "You had a magical explosion over a bunny?"

His arms fell. "What? Did Page tell you that? How did he know?"

He? I asked Page.

Yes, 'he' is fine, and tell Ryland I hear all the gossip.

"Page says he hears all the gossip."

Ryland craned his neck to look at the ceiling far above. "You didn't have to tell her I'm afraid of rabbits!"

I chuckled, and color sprang into each strip of wood and rug between me and Ryland. "Afraid? As in present tense? Interesting."

Sylvie patted his arm. "It's okay, dear. Even MBI detectives can have phobias."

He muttered something under his breath just as Page said, *I've missed having life within these walls.* He let out another sigh.

My breath caught. This wonderful being, this miracle of life, was alone and dying.

Anyway, you misunderstood me before. Our bond would hone your magic, not amplify it. If you seek control, this will help. I can show you. Close your eyes, Page said. When I didn't, he added, *Trust me.*

After a quick look at Ryland and Sylvie, I let my eyelids fall.

I thought Page's voice had twined its way into my mind already, but now he punctured my bones and blew through my emotional armor. For someone who'd kept others at a distance for over two decades, the sensation should have felt odd. I should have rejected it, held it at bay like I had even my fiancé—which is probably why I hadn't realized he was a pus-filled, festering wound ready to pop.

But I didn't want to reject Page. I felt like I'd curled up in front of a fire after years of being lost in the snowy woods. Page saw all of me, and it felt right. An old friend—no, family—finally calling me home.

I felt him too now. Months of grief and loneliness. Years of love and connection with my grandmother, whose laugh I could feel as it rode some current between me and Page. Unfettered joy at putting the book each human needed, really needed, in their hands. Maybe they came in for a self-help book and left with one about the courage to get a divorce. Maybe they came in for the latest high-brow literary title and left with a hilarious rom-com. They always got what they needed, which gave Page what he needed.

And beneath all that emotion, I sensed my magic. Clear. Settled. A pond of peonies I could dip my wand into any time I needed.

You can really help keep me from demolishing anything? I asked.

I'd serve as an anchor *for you. We can only communicate within a short range of the shop, but even outside of that range, the bond would anchor you.*

Releasing a relieved breath, I smiled. *So, what book does my soul need right now, Page?*

A puff of rippling papers teased my mind. *Kinley, you already know, but only you can accept it.*

I watched my magic swirl, content and contained in its pool, let the warmth of it fill me.

Okay, Page. Let's bond.

Are you sure?

Page, I said, lowering my tone. *You already know.*

He tsked. *No need to mock me. Take a breath. Keep your eyes shut.*

I did as instructed. After a minute, I felt a dot of heat in the center of my forehead. Little molten offshoots seared me as they made their way across my face, my neck, my torso, and to my toes.

Just when I thought I couldn't take it anymore, the fire faded to feathers, like floating on clouds. Page settled around me again, just like before, only now I could sense a link between us. Something that could never be broken, never be taken from me.

Opening my eyes, I looked around at the fully revitalized, dazzling bookshop, and smiled at the overflowing shelves. My soul sang, because it didn't need *one* book. It needed *all* the books. And now it had them.

I pushed to my feet, only to promptly tumble back into the chair. Sylvie and Ryland rushed forward. "Are you okay?" Ryland asked. "You almost look worse than earlier."

"Oh, thanks." I put a hand on my forehead. "Just a little dizzy."

It's a side effect of the bonding. Don't worry, it will pass.

I repeated Page's words to my companions and stood again, despite their protests. "I have plenty of experience with dizziness, thank you very much." That had been the migraine symptom to embarrass Aaron the night before.

But I was going to look at my bookstore, no matter how unbalanced I felt.

The same almost-emerald as the armchair had painted the walls all the way to the exposed wood ceiling above the second floor. A green two shades darker had invaded the rugs, with a pattern of light green vines connecting little golden books. The cherry floors beneath blended right in with all the bookcases and display tables.

Taking careful steps, I moved through the store, passing a plume of colorful books, their pages whispering to me as I passed. I didn't have to run my fingers over the foiled jacket of a hardcover to know how it felt, just like I knew how soft the velvet pillow resting in a chair would be or how the springs would squeak when a customer sat down. I approached the long, deep sales counter in the center of the store, certain the marble top would feel warmer than expected.

Pausing, I let myself breathe in the scent of fresh paper, let the taste of ink wash over my tongue. Page claimed every inch of this store, knew it down to its every atom, and now I did too.

I continued on to the staircase, letting out a little squeak when I spotted the front of the steps. Each step looked like a pile of old books. As I watched, the titles shifted, the colors changed. "This is so cool!"

Thank you, Page said.

"It's my favorite part too," Ryland told me. "Though, I also love the themed sections, and the—"

Ryland took a step back as a book whacked him lightly in the face. The spine read *Quiet*. "Umm, okay, Page."

Why? I asked, raising my eyebrow at the rafters.

I have much work to do before you see the entire store, Page told me. *Things to get in order tonight.*

I scrunched up my nose, and in my surprise, forgot to speak inside my mind. "You can change yourself around?"

To my left, a pile of books rearranged themselves into the word "Yes."

Can you do your own hair? Page asked. *Never mind. Clearly not. Look at it.*

Grabbing a tangle, I said, "Hey! Have a little sympathy. I was supposed to get married today."

A book flew up to me. *Hairstyles 101.*

I crossed my arms. "Very funny."

Ryland's lips quirked. "I like your hair. It's got a toddler-who-cut-their-own-hair vibe."

Sylvie smacked his arm. "It does not."

"Thank—" I started to say, but Sylvie cut me off.

"It's more '80s rock star who hasn't washed their hair in a month."

I glowered at the pair of them. "Well, then, I guess I better go wash it, since Page doesn't want me to see the rest of the store."

Ryland looked around. "I wonder if he'll just reorganize or do a grand theme. The tourists love the themes." The glint in his eyes told me he loved them too.

"Does Sea Sprite get a lot of tourists?" I asked as we walked toward the door.

"Yes. We have a portal system that connects the magical towns." Sylvie looked at me out of the corner of her eye. "Having the entire island to ourselves is a rarity. Most other magical towns are just a piece of hidden land." I had so many questions, but my brain couldn't handle more answers.

Sylvie continued, "Tourists come here for the island, and for many of our businesses, but quite a few come for Page specifically."

"He's famous. Entirely unique," Ryland said. "Our economy has taken a dip the last couple months."

I froze a few feet from the door. "So, if I hadn't arrived and bonded with Page, the town would have suffered? Why didn't you tell me?"

Sylvie shrugged. "We didn't want to influence you too much."

After taking a breath to counteract a fresh wave of light-headedness, I said to the rafters, "Well, it's a good thing I wasn't about to let a majestic bookshop like you die, Page. I'll see you tomorrow."

Take care of yourself, Kinley.

As the floor vibrated and I sensed books tumbling around in the depths of the store, I said, "I'll be okay. I'm pretty sure things can't possibly get any worse."

Chapter Six

"It's so...big. My grandma lived here all alone?"

Sylvie nodded. "Generations of your family have lived here, often many at one time, but your family has dwindled in recent decades." She lifted a hand. "Shall we?"

I hoisted my tote bag farther up my shoulder and took small steps down a steep brick path to the massive Victorian home below us. My arches felt like they'd collapse any second, and the tips of my toes had numbed. Sylvie kept close with her wand out, as if sensing I might fall. A paper bag stamped with The Moon Bear's Oven floated at her side.

I'd wanted to come straight here to shower, but Sylvie had insisted I eat dinner. She'd noticed me eying the Indian

restaurant earlier, so we'd eaten there. Sylvie had ordered
an entrée and two appetizers to take her husband, who
she'd said would never forgive her if she didn't bring him
something from his favorite restaurant.

My grandmother's house sat just above the beach. It had
grown dark, so I couldn't see the waves, but I could hear
them whispering on the far side of the expansive lawn.

We hadn't walked far to get here—just down Double,
Double Street, past Trouble Avenue, up a hill, and past a
few other residential streets.

I paused again at the bottom of the path to take in
the light blue house with black shutters. Several outdoor
lamps had powered on when we'd stepped within six feet.
I'd read about houses like this countless times in books.
Imagined being swept away from the foster system and
into a world of fresh cookies made in a gigantic kitchen,
hidden crawlspaces full of wondrous secrets, and bay windows stuffed with pillows you could read on for hours. I
spotted such a window just to the right of the front door.
The house of my dreams had existed all along, complete
with a grandmother who'd wanted me.

I sighed and climbed the white stairs onto the wraparound porch overflowing with a riot of plants, some of
which slithered and crawled up the siding and along the
planks beneath us. "Of course the plants move."

"You'll get used to it." Sylvie took out the key ring she'd
used to unlock the bookshop and offered it to me. "The
smaller key fits the house."

My breath hitched. An entire house that could fit at least three houses inside it, just for me. If the state of my feet hadn't meant I'd have to fly back up that hill on a broomstick in order to run away—and no way in a mermaid's mane was I getting on one of those death traps—I might have done it, but I took the key.

Upon stepping closer, I realized the black door had tiny stars moving slowly across it. Would magic ever cease to amaze me?

The key turned with a snick, and I opened the door. Soft lighting filled the long hall. "Here goes nothing." I stepped onto the oak floors.

Flipping from foster home to foster home had honed my eye. The first five minutes in someone's residence told me everything I needed to know.

At twelve, I'd known from the crammed bookshelves, quilting supplies, and the plate of brownies waiting for me in Mrs. Winkel's living room that we'd be fast friends.

At thirteen, after she'd had to move in with her son and I'd arrived at the Johansson house, I'd known after ten seconds that I'd be safe there but very annoyed. Portraits of every senator from Wisconsin ever to serve hung all over their walls, which Scott and Misty told me *all* about in those first ten seconds. They'd never traveled to Wisconsin, and as far as they knew, neither had any of their friends or family. The Johanssons just found the state's politics fascinating, and they reminded me at length over breakfast. Every. Day.

Now, as I absorbed my grandmother's living room to the right—which the house so kindly lit for me—I knew four things. Photo frames on the mantle and tables told me how she adored her family. Quilts and throw pillows stacked on the blue couch and four armchairs told me she loved comfort. Little signs with sayings like "I'm the Wicked Witch of Everything" told me she had a sense of humor. And she loved sunflowers. They'd been stitched into the quilts and throw pillows. Painted onto the signs. Carved into the photo frames.

But beyond all that, I knew we'd have filled this house with so much love and laughter if we'd been given the chance.

With my chest aching, I ran my fingers over a needlepoint sunflower hanging next to a stuffed bookcase—because of course she had books everywhere too. Overflowing shelves in the corners and a whole wall of books surrounding the fireplace.

"Just wait until you see the sunflower garden," Sylvie said. She picked up a photo and handed it to me. A woman with red hair and a radiant smile standing amidst sunflowers twice her small stature.

"This is Margaret?"

"Yes."

I looked at her a minute longer until a tapping noise made me jolt and almost lose my dinner.

"That's just Mark," Sylvie said.

"Someone lives here?"

She winked. "Yep." Sylvie led me down the hall to an atrium that soared through the second story to the night sky beyond. And there, tapping on the glass, was Mark the sunflower.

"The first sunflower Margaret ever planted. He's been sad without her, so take good care of him."

I crossed my arms. "First, a sentient bookshop. Now, a sentient sunflower?"

With a laugh, she waved me off. "He's not sentient, just...aware."

"Great. On that note, I'm going to find the bathroom. Thanks for all your help today."

"You don't want a tour?"

"Naw. I need time alone." She looked wary of leaving me, so I smiled. "The kid in me desperately wants to explore this place on my own. I'm ninety-nine percent sure there's a secret passageway, and I'm going to find it."

Sylvie's eyes twinkled, but she neither affirmed nor denied. "If you need anything, you can ask your neighbors in the yellow house, Sundar and Miguel. They're wonderful. Get some rest, honey."

After I thanked her profusely, I shut the door and leaned against it. A deep breath brought me the house's soothing lavender scent. I could feel the precious memories here, but I couldn't get over the size and how much *stuff* it contained.

My place in Portland took minimalism to the extreme, so this place overwhelmed me.

I kicked off my heels. "Okay, Kinley, how overwhelming can the bathroom be?"

Worst question ever.

Oak doors lined both sides of the upstairs hallway, except for one curious door at the very end that had been painted to look like a book cover with a forest scene. "*Lost in Sea Sprite Wood* by E. L. Sylvain," I read aloud to no one...unless you counted Mark.

I gingerly opened the door, half expecting another portal to take me to Narnia but found a wide bathroom.

As my bare foot hit the tile, the room illuminated. "Whoa." A standalone tub formed entirely of books, inside and out, took center stage in the room. On the ivory walls around it, black lines of text popped up one letter at a time. When the walls filled, they went blank and the unseen typewriter began again. The sight entranced me, made more captivating by a soundtrack of turning book pages.

I dropped my tote onto a vanity painted with a thousand bookmarks and made straight for the tub. I reached for the faucet, expecting to find a handle of some sort...you know, like every other bathroom on the planet. Nope. I looked up. The ceiling had a showerhead, but no controls. I searched the walls and all four sides of the tub. Nothing.

Leaning over the tub, I raised my arms. "Water!" No water. "Shower, I command thee to flow!" Fail. I kept trying more ridiculous phrases, finally giving up at "Oh, great lords of magic, I beg of you to please let thine cleansing waters gush so I can wash off the stench of Aaron, the human cockroach."

I sat on the tub, debating taking a bath in the ocean. I smacked my hand on the side. "Why won't you turn on?"

And, of course, that's when the faucet sputtered.

It took me twenty minutes to get the tub to do what I wanted—stopper and fill with actual hot water, not the freezing water it insisted on—while also trying to remove my wedding dress by myself. I really could have used another magical explosion.

Eventually, I took the most soothing bath of my life, even taking a guess that the tub would give me bubble bath if I asked correctly.

The water never lost its warmth, so I considered sleeping there, but I forced myself out after what seemed like hours. I grabbed a towel that smelled like new books and felt fresh out of the dryer, reminding me of how Ryland's magic had felt as it swept through me back in the bridal suite.

I walked down the hallway, hair dripping behind me, finding more rooms full of too much stuff until I came to a room with a white four-poster bed, blue patchwork quilt, and blissfully bare dresser and nightstand.

Still wrapped in the towel, I crawled into the cold sheets, and dreamed of a cloud of pink marshmallows carrying me to a meadow where I tucked myself onto a lilac gumdrop and read about fairies, while—across from me, on a coral gumdrop—a blond man stroked a tiny black dragon as he read *The Hobbit*.

"Why are you doing this to me, Witchuccino 5000?"

I smacked the side of the machine, wincing as the bright morning rays reflected off the stainless steel accents. Even when I didn't have a migraine, sharp slivers of light like those bouncing off the uncooperative coffee maker spiked a fear response. That's right, the very concept of *sunlight* scared me.

"Okay, listen. I had the longest day ever yesterday, so please, for the love of broomsticks or wands or whatever form of magic you find most captivating, please give me a cup of coffee. Or a cappuccino. Or an espresso. Heck, I'd take a half-caf mocha supreme raspberry extra sludgey latte with a twist. Actually, that won't work. Full caffeine is required."

I'd slept for a solid eight hours, not waking once. But given the emotional turmoil of yesterday and the night I'd spent traipsing around in heels *after* running around all day to ensure my wedding to that talking turd would go off without a hitch—which it did, we did not get hitched—eight hours didn't cut it.

And now I'd discovered that the Witchuccino 5000, of course, ran on magic. "Fine, no mocha sludge either." I hadn't been able to find any buttons on the machine, but maybe I needed to tweak one of the spouts. With two fingers, I unscrewed and rescrewed a tiny steel pipe. Raising my voice so it carried through my grandma's cozy kitchen, rebounding off the yellow walls and many white cabinets, I yelled, "GIVE ME AN ESPRESSO BEFORE I CHUCK YOU IN THE OCEAN!"

The machine chugged to life, and I whooped, but my happy dance turned to a quick step to the sink after the Witchuccino 5000 squirted scalding espresso all over the chunky gray sweater I wore.

Luckily, the sink worked with a standard faucet, and I got cool water on the affected skin quickly. Not much espresso had penetrated the thick knit I'd found in my grandma's closet. The sweater was comfy, as were the flowy pants and tank top I'd found. A few inches of ankle showed at the bottom of the pants, but I didn't give a bat's butt. I hadn't worn something this forgiving in years.

I bent over to inspect the spout. What had I done to make it shoot espresso up instead of down? "At least it didn't cover me with milk."

A dust-gray cat jumped onto the counter next to me, and my heart tried to burst through my ribs as it squealed, "Oooooh, that's a cool toy!"

"*Cool...toy*," I repeated, clutching my heaving chest.

"Dispensing *cool soy* milk," my nemesis coffee maker said a second before it shot said liquid into my gaping mouth.

I sputtered and stepped back. A frickin' talking cat sat before me, swishing its tail and looking more enthused than I'd ever felt.

"Nice! You caught all the milk. That's a neat trick." The cat began bobbing on her toes. "Oh my god, I love your plaid top. You look like Cher!"

Still spinning on the whole talking cat thing, my brain didn't process her words for a full ten seconds. "The...sin ger?"

The cat straightened. "As if!"

My fingers plucked at the yellow plaid tank top I wore beneath the chunky cardigan. "Oh, you mean Cher from the movie *Clueless*?" The shirt reminded me of her legendary yellow plaid skirt.

"Yes!" The cat's eyes glowed. "I knew you'd get me. But before we have girl time and do makeovers, there's something you should see first."

The talking cat wanted to do makeovers? Sure, why not. I already had a sentient bookstore and a semi-sentient sunflower. Why not a super-sentient, talking cat who wanted me to paint her toenails?

She turned and walked down the counter toward the front of the kitchen. I ran after her. "Wait! Where are you going? How did you get in here? Who are you?"

"I came in through the back doors." Right. I'd thrown open the wide double doors at the back of the kitchen, eager to hear the waves lapping against the rocks below, but I'd tuned them out in my quest for coffee. "And I'm Twilight, but we can gab like gal pals later. C'mon."

Twilight hopped off the counter and darted between my legs. I raced after her, down the long hall, past Mark's atrium and several rooms I'd yet to explore.

She paused at the front door. "Okay, so like, take a deep breath."

"What? Why?"

"Trust me." Then she jumped up, landed on the handle, flicked the deadbolt, and lowered the lever handle.

The door swung open, Twilight diving off just as I got my first view of what awaited me.

A scream tore from me, echoing through the house.

When I finally caught my breath, I took several cautious steps forward on tiptoes, as if not squeaking a floorboard was vitally important when approaching a dead body.

Because there, on the shiny white planks of the porch, lay my grouchy tenant, Denise. Her chest still, her eyes unblinking. Lined journal pages had been stuffed down her throat. Just like I'd threatened the day before.

Chapter Seven

"So, do we need to call the police or something? Because when Cher got robbed in *Clueless*—"

"Are you okay?" a deep voice called.

I spun to find two men jogging toward me from the house next door—a smaller version of my grandmother's with pale yellow siding and green shutters. A shaggy golden dog bounded in front of the men, taking the steps two at a time.

"Oh my cauldrons, I love dogs!" Twilight said, rushing over to greet the creature.

I just stared as they sniffed each other inches from *Denise's dead body.*

The stairs creaked as the men joined us. The first slammed to a stop when he saw the very stationary stationery-store owner, causing the second to run into his back.

Slowly, the tall South Asian man's copper eyes lifted to mine. "Are you okay?"

"Yes. I just found her a minute ago."

A vine from a nearby plant slithered across the porch, poked Denise's shoe, and retreated.

"Actually, I found her!" Twilight said, bouncing on her toes.

The men didn't react to her words as the second, slightly shorter Latino man stepped around the first. "Oh no." He crouched down to press two fingers to Denise's pulse point. After a few seconds, he shook his head, confirming what I already knew.

He slipped a phone out of his pocket and stepped away to call the police.

My stomach roiled, and a wave of dizziness made me rock from side to side. I was suddenly thankful I hadn't had any coffee.

The first man took my arm and guided me to a pair of black Adirondack chairs in the far corner of the wraparound porch. He dragged them so Denise wouldn't be visible.

I sat and wrapped my arms around myself. "Thank you."

"Of course. You must be Kinley. Sylvie texted us yesterday." He leaned back, the sun catching half his face, lighting up his bronze skin. "I'm Sundar. That's my husband, Miguel."

"Oh! Sylvie told me yesterday that your parents own The Moon Bear's Oven. We ate there last night. I loved it."

I felt weird complimenting a restaurant just then, but the last twenty-four hours had been an episode of *The Twilight Zone*, so why not?

"It is delicious," he said. "I'm sorry your introduction to our world has been so...challenging. We heard a bit about yesterday, and now this."

I sighed. "Yep. Not ideal."

Twilight, the overgrown golden retriever, and Miguel approached. "The police will be here any—" Miguel startled as a portal opened two inches from him. He dove out of the way right before Ryland stepped through.

The detective took a minute to assess the scene, his eyes resting on me for a beat, before he copied Miguel by taking Denise's pulse. "I need you all to move to the yard. Familiars too."

I shivered as my feet hit the dewy grass. Twilight leaned against my ankle, and if I hadn't been cold, I'd have shaken her off. Cats had never liked me, so having one follow me and gaze up at me with wide, adoring eyes felt strange. Why hadn't she left yet?

Miguel stood across from me, running his fingers down the dog's back and telling her, "I know. It's okay to feel sad."

"Ah," I said. "Is she your familiar?"

He smiled. "Yes, this is Dawn."

I gave her a little wave, and she held up a paw.

Miguel ran his hands over the tawny skin of his arms. "I should have grabbed a sweater, but we heard you cry out as we were coming downstairs and didn't stop." He pulled out a green wand with a shining blue handle and muttered something. A few seconds later, a sweatshirt sailed out of the yellow house.

"Whoa." I needed to learn that spell immediately.

Sundar laughed. "It will be fun to watch you learn about magic," he said, as if he planned to be in my life.

Did neighbors do that here?

"So fun!" Twilight agreed.

Erm, okay? Her too?

"Do you want me to summon you a jacket, babe?" Miguel asked Sundar as his head popped out of his sweatshirt, his short black hair mussed.

Sundar flicked his eyes to the porch. "No, I think the cold is helping keep me sane right now."

Ryland came down the stairs. "Can I have a minute with Kinley?"

My neighbors stepped aside, but Twilight stayed. She sniffed Ryland's sneakers—the same shoes as yesterday but dyed royal-blue.

"How are you?" Ryland asked, lowering his voice.

I shrugged. "Feeling a bit unmoored. Wondering how Denise ended up on my porch. Trying not to hurl."

He squeezed my shoulder. "Hang in there. I'll do my best to hold off my superiors, but so many people heard you argue with Denise yesterday."

Nausea clutched at my empty stomach again. "Oh, I know. I threatened to choke her with a journal, and here she is, dead on my porch with journal pages crammed into her mouth. You know I didn't do this, right?"

We'd met only the afternoon before, and I hadn't been the definition of grace and poise, but I hadn't given off murderer vibes, right?

"If you were going to kill anyone, I'm pretty sure it would be that nitwit Aaron. Besides, Page wouldn't bond a murderer. But it doesn't look good, Kinley."

An hour later, Sundar and Miguel led me into Mystic Mugs, the coffee shop next door to my bookstore. The rest of Ryland's team had arrived moments after he warned me that everyone would think I killed Denise. They'd taken our statements and then kicked us out. Ryland had grabbed my tote bag for me for the second time in two days.

The whirring espresso machine, murmuring crowd, and laughing babies immediately relaxed me. I knew these sounds, understood the layout of the many black tables scattered across the painted-concrete floors, recognized the exposed rafters, and the chalkboard menu. Mystic Mugs looked like dozens of coffee shops I'd visited.

With a relieved sigh, I stepped into the short line.

"Why don't you sit?" Miguel said, looping his arm through mine and guiding me to a corner table. My heels clacked as we walked. I'd tried to slip my feet into my grandmother's shoes that morning, but they didn't fit, so Ryland had needed to grab my torturous wedding heels from inside the *crime scene.*

Dawn and Twilight followed us, the canine curling up under the table while the feline jumped on top. I guess the town's food safety regulations accommodated familiars and talking cats, since I also saw a parrot and a ferret in the shop. Miguel went to join Sundar in line.

"Okay, Twilight," I said. "Why are you here?"

She cocked her head. "Because you are."

"And why are you going where I go?"

She leaned toward me. "Is this a prank? Because I'm totally here for it. I love pranks! Dawn, does Miguel prank you?"

The gears finally shifted into place. "Hexes." I rubbed below my left eyebrow, just inside my nose. "You're my familiar."

"Of course! How else could you hear me talk?"

"You'll have to forgive me. I don't know my foot from my ear in this world." Not only that, but Twilight's voice didn't sound like Page's. When Page had spoken the day before, I knew only I could hear him. His voice unfolded from deep within me. Twilight sounded like any other external voice, even though her words were apparently only for me.

Twilight swished her tail. "That's okay. I've been waiting *decades* for you, so now I'm the best trained familiar in the country. I'll help you."

"Decades?"

"Witches typically get their familiars between the ages of thirteen and sixteen, once both are mature enough. But you, ah, never had your magic."

I clutched my sweater. "You've waited all this time?"

"What else would I do?"

Sundar set down two cups while Miguel plopped a heap of pastries on the table.

"I think I'm in love with you both," I said, salivating over a chocolate-chip muffin.

"You might want to send some of that love over here," a beaming Latina woman said. "Because I made your drink."

Her long, wavy black hair caught the light as she leaned down to place two steaming cups on the table. She smiled. "I'm Zoriana, but most people call me Zori." The shorter of the two cups hit at the wrong angle and tipped, black liquid sloshing out. "Conjured cosmos!"

Twilight rushed over to steady the cup with her paw.

"She's my niece," Miguel said as he and his husband sat on either side of me. "My clumsy niece."

I looked between them. Miguel couldn't be past his late thirties, while Zori looked to be a few years younger than me.

Zori chuckled as she pulled off her black Mystic Mugs apron, the strings catching on her emerald, dolman-sleeve sweater. "We're only ten years apart, so we're more like cousins." Looking at her watch, she took the fourth chair. "I have fifteen minutes. Don't let me forget to get back up!"

Miguel ruffled her hair. "I got you, don't worry."

"So," Zori said, turning to me with a frown on her round face. "I hear you've had a rough couple days." She pointed to the cup in front of me. "That should help."

I raised a brow. "Because caffeine is one of the world's greatest treasures?"

She chuckled. "Yes, but also because I mixed in a calming tonic. The owner creates genius tonics that taste divine and give beverages a boost. Oh, the drink has a hefty dose of chocolate too."

I snatched the cup like it was the Holy Grail and took a sip. I melted into the chair like the chocolate in my coffee. This wasn't a few pumps of mocha syrup—this was freshly melted deliciousness. I downed half the cup.

"Can I have some?" Twilight asked.

"Absolutely not!" I told her, clutching desperately to my cup. She looked so sad, though, that I reached out and patted her on the head.

"Do you feel calmer?" Sundar asked as he sipped his iced coffee.

"Yes, thank you all so much." I reached for the muffin I'd been eyeing. "May I?"

"Please," Miguel said. "We bought one of everything."

I tore open the plastic and devoured it, grateful my nausea had eased with the calming tonic.

"What happened with Denise yesterday?" Zori asked, picking pieces off a blueberry scone.

I launched into the story. A couple tables filled in around us as I spoke, so I lowered my voice as I told them about how my empty threat had been carried out by someone.

"They actually stuffed journal pages down her throat?" Zori said, her voice nowhere near as quiet as mine. Several heads turned. "Oh, sorry! I get carried away sometimes."

"Speaking of," Miguel said. "You have less than one minute left."

Zori jumped up, smacking her knee into the table. "Ouch!"

Sundar grabbed her wrist. "You're coming to dinner tonight, right?"

She tugged on one of her waves. "Of course! I totally remembered we're having dinner tonight. I'll be there at five."

He chuckled. "Six."

"That's what I said." Zori hustled into her apron and sped behind Mystic Mugs' counter.

"Excuse me," a white woman of about seventy at the next table said. "My apologies. I couldn't help but overhear."

Sundar nodded. "That's okay, Martha. I didn't notice you there. This is Kinley Paigewright. Margaret's granddaughter." He looked at me. "This is Martha Malfina, the best seer in town, and Denise's neighbor."

Seer...as in the future?

Martha shook her head, a small strand of gray hair freeing itself from her bun. "If only I'd seen this coming. I told Denise that I saw a bleak ending if she didn't change her ways, but the vision lacked any detail. Denise didn't listen to me, and now look. She kept treating people poorly, like she did to you yesterday, Kinley."

The calming tonic in my veins evaporated. "Wait, I didn't kill her! She was rude to me, but I would never hurt someone."

Martha reached over to pat my hand, just barely touching her fingers to mine. "Of course, dear. Only the gullible will believe you killed her. Clearly, someone saw your argument and used it to cover their tracks."

"But some people will believe I'm the killer." I took another gulp of coffee.

Miguel twisted in his chair to see Martha better. "Do you know anyone who would want to hurt Denise?"

I perked up. As her neighbor, would Martha know anything?

"Not specifically. Well, the entire neighborhood disliked Denise. She kept her lawn perfect and harshly judged anyone who didn't. She always watched. Sneered at others over every fallen leaf. But inside her house? She hoarded. I could see it through the windows. Stuff everywhere. No wonder her husband left her. When he moved out, he took almost nothing. It's all hers."

Annoyed neighbors. An ex-husband.

"Can you think of anything else?" I asked.

Martha shook her head. "No. I'll let you know if I do." She zipped up her red fleece jacket and gave me a reassuring smile. "I need to get going." With her coffee cup in hand, she stood and took a few steps. "Actually..."

I straightened.

"A few months back, Denise had a broken wrist. She wouldn't tell anyone what happened. The healers couldn't mend it instantly. It had to heal over a few *days*. Denise tried to hide it from everyone, but I saw it."

Sundar's brows pinched. "That's so odd."

"Most unusual," Martha agreed before she left.

Interesting. A mysterious broken wrist. I'd learned a lot about Denise in the last five minutes.

I tapped my stiletto, careful not to step on Dawn's tail. Ryland seemed like a competent detective, but I'd clung to my self-reliance for decades, and I wasn't about to loosen my grip while suspected of murder. Could I find out more about Denise, something to take the target off my back?

Downing the rest of my coffee, I stood. I knew what to do.

Chapter Eight

"Wow! It's so spacious. So green. And kinda pink? I love pink!" Twilight's ears twitched as she spun in circles to take in The Perfect Page.

The door closed behind me with a small click, and I gave a little spin myself. "You're right." Pink had invaded the space somehow, giving everything a slight rosy tinge.

I have coated the windows with FL-41 technology that blocks the wavelengths of light most likely to aggravate your migraines, as your pink glasses do, Page said. *I used specifications I found on the internet.*

Of course the sentient bookshop had internet access.

My eyes burned. No one had ever considered my migraines to be anything but a nuisance. Not my coworkers, not Aaron. No one had tried to help me with them. *Thank you, Page. This means everything to me.*

"That's so kind of you!" Twilight said.

A floorboard squeaked as I paused on my way to the sales counter. "Wait, you can hear Page?"

I'd explained all about the sentient bookstore while we'd made a pit stop. Sundar and Miguel had seemed surprised at my sudden desire to leave, so I'd told them I couldn't spend one more minute in my wedding heels. They'd given me directions to The Sorcerer's Shoe and made me promise to join them for dinner that night.

While I just stared at them in surprise—I wasn't used to nice neighbors—Twilight had danced around and mewed her excitement. Not wanting to disappoint her, I'd accepted.

I really had needed shoes, so my new familiar and I had walked over to Toil Avenue to try on footwear. Twilight instantly vetoed my usual "boring as barf" flats. She'd wanted me to get sparkly gold sneakers, which made me want to barf, so we'd compromised on a pair of black zip-up ankle boots.

Magic obviously had a lot of benefits, but the *shoes*. Not only had the witch proprietor—an object enchanter, he'd informed me—spelled them to fit my feet perfectly, they felt like walking on butter.

Our adventure had given me plenty of time to prepare Twilight for Page, but I hadn't expected her to hear him.

Of course she can hear me. As a Paigewright familiar, she has all the same privileges in this relationship as you and I.

I kept walking. *That's amazing.*

Yes, but she can't hear inside your *head.*

Right. "That's amazing, Twilight. I'm glad you can speak with Page too."

I set my tote bag and the shopping bag with my old, likely to-be-burned shoes on the long marble counter.

Your hair is acceptable today, though rather flat.

I snorted. "Sleep and wet hair don't mesh well, and my hair tools are back in Portland."

"It looks fabulous," Twilight said.

I winked at her. "Did you have fun rearranging, Page?"

Yes.

"I thought things would look a bit, erm, different in the store," I admitted. Other than the hibiscus hue, it looked the same.

A flurry of paper riding a fierce wind erupted in my mind.

Oops. "I'm not disappointed, though. The store is perfect!"

Page chuckled. *It's okay. I only meant to tease you. Most of the changes are not visible from here.*

I guess I could see some, then. Squinting, I finally noticed a few brick walls around the reading nooks. I walked closer to see random bricks painted to look like book spines.

Of my favorite books.

"Wands and willows!" Twilight cried from somewhere above.

I ran to the staircase, jogging up the first few steps.

She's fine. Just impressed by my creativity.

With a laugh, I slowed and took in the staircase as I ascended. Each step's facade of old books, the titles changing as I watched, looked so real that I could almost feel each cracked cover on my fingertips, but as Page's bonded witch, I recognized the illusion. Same with the spindles, which each appeared to be wrapped in book pages.

As my head crested the final stair, I froze. "Wands and willows, indeed." Part of the top floor was open to the shop below, with a balcony wrapping around, but the stacks beyond it had become a dim forest, crowded with wide tree trunks, their branches forming a dense canopy. Moss coated the cherry floors, leading me into the trees. I discovered shelves tucked between and inside the trunks, each one lit by a small light to highlight the titles within.

Twilight perched on a tree-stump ottoman that sat before an armchair cut from a boulder. I knew it would be high-quality memory foam, no matter how unforgiving it looked. A chorus of crickets joined our "oohs" and "aahs" as we discovered new things. A fox hiding between two stacks. A dragon clinging to a branch. An old log full of children's practice swords and bows.

And a treehouse in the corner of the ceiling, which Twilight immediately climbed into.

Do you like it? Page asked.

You know I do. It's magnificent.

I hadn't given a hoot about my wedding colors or centerpieces, but a thought hit me then: *This* is where I would get married.

I shook it off with a harsh reminder that I no longer had a fiancé.

Page called my attention to a particular vine-entwined table. Just like the bricks downstairs, it had all my favorite books. I brushed my fingers over a special edition of *The Lord of the Rings* before flitting them over a trove of other fantasy books.

I'd lied to Ryland when he'd first presented Midnight to me back at the bridal suite. I'd told him I didn't like fantasy and hadn't corrected the fib even when he'd told me about the books he'd read with his mom.

Or, you know, upon realizing he lived in a real fantasy world.

I loved fantasy, but I'd learned to hide it when Aaron and his family had looked at me like I'd grown a unicorn horn after I'd referred to *The Hobbit*. Perhaps my love of magic had helped me so readily accept this new world.

Thank you, Page. I put a hand on my heart. *Thank you.*

Of course. I look forward to creating more wondrous themes together. Now, I believe you came here today to ask me something.

I would have to work on not letting that creep me out.

Twilight came trotting over. "Yes! We're on a mission."

I couldn't help but smile at her enthusiasm. "Page, do we have a key to Denise's shop? I thought if I could get in there before the police, maybe I could find something to help clear my name. Technically, I own the property, so it wouldn't be breaking in, right? Wait, do you know about Denise?"

Twilight told me everything the instant you arrived, before I knew her name.

That sounded right.

"So, do we have a key?"

"It's in the office," a honeyed voice said behind me.

I whipped around, and as all the blood drained from my face, I knew I'd gone paler than the ghost in front of me. "You...I...dead." With a lurching step backward, I banged into the table. My feet tangled like the vines on the wood behind me, and I pitched to the left. Halfway to the ground, a pile of paperbacks caught me.

Thanks, Page.

The books pushed me to my feet, and the spectral Diane Keaton who'd scared me glided forward. She pushed up her round glasses and straightened the tie beneath her vest. "I'm so sorry. I didn't mean to scare you."

"Maybe I should have ascended first," a husky yet bright voice said, and I peered through the ghost to see a white woman stepping off the escalator. The cane in her hand—a beautiful transparent piece with tiny black birds diving gracefully through its depths—must have prompted Page to convert the stairs to an escalator. The ghost stepped back to allow the smirking woman to come forward, her cane nearly silent on the moss. Her juicy red curls and freckles made her look almost ethereal in the dim light, like she fit right into this forest fae setting, even though she didn't have any wings like Sea Sprite's actual fairies.

"I'm Shea." She pulled my hand into a firm shake. "This is Tansy, one of your grandmother's best friends for fifty years and my mentor."

Tansy tipped her bowler hat.

You could have told me someone had come into the shop, Page.

He huffed. *You could have locked the front door behind you, Kinley. Not that it would have stopped Tansy.*

Good point.

"Nice to meet you," I said, "though I'm still a little shocked about the whole ghost thing. Does everyone become a ghost? Is it a choice? Do you choose when to cross over? You know what, never mind." My brain couldn't handle more information.

"Introduce me!" Twilight said, bouncing on her paws again.

"Right, sorry. Tansy, Shea, meet Twilight."

Shea leaned down and scooped Twilight up with her free arm, tucking the cat against her curvy body. "Come here, you. I can't imagine what you've been through, waiting for your witch for so long."

Guilt prickled the base of my skull, and it must have shown on my face.

"It's not your fault," Tansy said. "I was there when your mother left, when we searched for you. This happened *to* you, not *because of* you, Kinley."

I nodded and averted my eyes, landing on Twilight purring against Shea's collarbone. Maybe I should hold her like that? I'd never had a pet before, much less a familiar.

"Have you really been in Portland your entire life?" Tansy whispered.

"Yes. I ended up in the foster system after someone left me at a fire station. For the first nine years, I lived with the same family. The—"

"Huberts," Shea said, the gold rim around her blue eyes shining, "who lived on White Oak Trail."

I bit the inside of my cheek. "Are you a seer or a stalker?"

She laughed, the sound drifting into the trees. "I'm a shifter. A raven shifter." She stepped into my personal space. "I used to spend summers in Portland with my aunt who lived on White Oak Trail in a blue bungalow next door to a white house with yellow shutters and a matching—"

"Front door. A yellow front door. You're *that* Shea." I reached up and tugged on one of her curls, just like I used to do as a kid, always so enthralled when it bounced right back.

She released another full laugh. "We played every summer until you were just gone one year."

I felt Page wrap around my mind like a warm hug. Twilight squirmed until Shea passed her to me. I held the feline awkwardly for a moment until she burrowed into my neck.

That felt...*nice*.

"Umm, the Huberts died in a car accident. They were only in their sixties." I pressed Twilight closer and tightened my abs. I hadn't spoken about the Huberts in years. "It was...tragic. I had to go to a new foster home, and I bounced between placements and group homes after that."

Shea squeezed my shoulder. "Ah, muffin, I'm sorry. I had no idea you were a witch, much less a Paigewright, or I would have told someone."

A long tear lit up Tansy's ethereal face. "You never should have been away from Sea Sprite."

After a steadying breath, I said, "Well, I've been here about five seconds now, and I'm already a murder suspect, so we'll see how Sea Sprite works out for me. Is the prison on the island, or will they portal me to the mainland?"

Shea put a hand on her hip. "I'm sorry. What the spell did you just say?"

I filled them in on Denise's death. "So, after everything I learned in the coffee shop, I got the idea to go check her business upstairs. I should probably hurry, though. If the police here are anything like in the human world, they'll want to block off her shop soon."

"I'll show you the key," Tansy said, wasting no time. She floated to the escalator. I let Shea step on first, following her with Twilight still pressed to my neck. At the bottom, Tansy turned behind the staircase. I followed, but did a double take when I spotted something glowing in an armchair.

"Oh, that's just Carl, my corgi familiar."

Ghost familiar? Why not.

The office sat inside a massive storeroom at the back of the shop, which Page assured me I'd never have to organize. He did all the inventory and book shuffling. Thank frick.

Page popped the safe and floated the key to me. I set Twilight down and took it.

"Wait," Tansy said. "In case the police have already arrived or anything, ah, untoward has occurred, let me scope things out." She zipped through the ceiling, her wide-legged khakis rippling.

"Was she a big *Annie Hall* fan?" I asked Shea.

She chuckled. "Not especially, but she needed a costume for a big party on Halloween 1977, the year *Annie Hall* premiered. Halloween's a big deal in our world, but she'd gotten caught up with work and hadn't planned anything, so she went with something quick and easy. The night didn't go well..."

I winced. "Now she's stuck wearing a bowler hat for eternity. It could be worse. She could have been a giant lobster."

"Or Chewbacca," Tansy said, floating down. "*Star Wars* came out that year too."

"So furry." I shuddered.

"It's all clear above."

"Okay, thank you." I gestured toward the front of the shop. "I'm glad to have met you both, but I need to show you out now."

Shea scoffed. "Do you think we're letting you snoop up there alone?" She snatched the key from me. "Let's go."

Chapter Nine

Before I could protest, Shea flung open the shop's back door. I hurried behind and emerged into an alley with a large brick building on the other side. A staircase led up to Denise's shop. Shea pushed a button, and it silently turned into an escalator. She waved me on, Twilight jumping up beside me.

The step took us two floors up to a little balcony. Shea strode to a heavy door, her cane clanging on the metal beneath us. She unlocked the door a second later, and we walked inside the stationery store, lit by Tansy's soft glow from where she waited a few feet inside.

Sparse seemed like a good word for Denise's storeroom. It held a few sets of supplies and tools, like ink and paper cutters, but the echo as the door shut and the small mounds of stock made me think the stationery store didn't move a lot of product.

Tansy seemed to read my mind. "I think she made most of her money off wedding invitations and programs. Denise enchanted objects and preferred to work with paper. She could make your wedding programs sing and dance and slap your guests if you wanted."

With a sigh, I ran my finger over a stack of ivory cardstock. "If only my box of unused wedding programs could take turns slapping my ex across the face. Maybe add in some paper cuts."

"Yes!" Twilight said. "And the paper can curl up and wedge underneath his fingernails."

My nose twitched as I regarded my familiar with a new terrified respect. I relayed her suggestion to the others.

"I'm sure we can arrange that and more," Shea said. "What's his address?"

Tansy shook her head. "Do you want to get thrown in jail, Shea?"

"No, but I can send him one of those human-world glitter bombs that bursts into tiny pieces he'll never get out of his hair, ears, and nose." She winked at me.

Twilight jumped onto Shea's shoulder. "Please make it pink glitter."

"My familiar would like pink glitter," I said, reaching over to run my fingers down her back.

"You got it, kitten," Shea said. "We'll discuss more details later. Let's search."

We split up. Shea stayed in the storeroom, carefully sifting through boxes. Tansy and I exited to the front, where Denise had long counters with glass enclosures showcasing some of her finest magic, as well as samples of paper, ink, ribbon, and other accessories.

Tansy wanted me and Twilight to search Denise's office while she took this room, as not only did she have the greatest understanding of magic, she could stick her head into the locked cabinets. But I couldn't help lollygagging on my way to the corner office.

A tall pillar with a glass cube atop it displayed a pale yellow box the size of a photograph. A sky-blue ribbon unfurled as I watched, and two flaps opened. A piece of cardstock arose and a heartbeat filled the air. Cursive script written by an invisible pen invited the viewer to a baby shower. When the last word dried, the ink washed away, replaced with a moving ultrasound image. Even through the glass, I could smell baby powder.

"Whoa," Twilight said. "That's impressive."

With a nod, I said, "Too bad Denise was so harsh."

"It did lose her a lot of customers," Tansy said from inside a display of engagement party invites.

I padded over to shelves of ready-to-purchase items, including quite a few stationery sets, pens, and, of course, journals. "Do you think one of these journals ended up down her throat?" I asked.

"We'd have to run inventory," Twilight said. When I gave her a funny look, she added, "What? I know about business. I've seen movies."

"C'mon." I waved her on, and we entered Denise's office, our path lit by cracked wooden blinds. A deep oak desk occupied most of the room, with an ergonomic chair behind it. Two plastic chairs sat before it, likely for customers to use while placing their orders. A few oak filing cabinets lined a side wall, but otherwise, the room felt quite bare.

"Back at the coffee shop, didn't Martha Malfina say Denise hoarded?" I asked my familiar.

Twilight hopped onto a chair and vaulted to the desk. "She did. I guess she only did that at home."

Minimalism at work, maximalism at home. We all had our contradictions.

I sat down, assuming I'd find a laptop in the desk drawers, but I found no technology at all. "She didn't even have a phone in here, much less a computer."

Twilight, who had her head in an open drawer, said, "Some magicals prefer to track things with magic instead of technology. Others use a combination."

"So Denise might have a magical database hidden in the literal clouds or something?"

My familiar looked up and tilted her head. "No, silly, the magic would record transactions on paper, which makes sense, given her love of paper."

"Oh! Right. I saw some books down here." From the bottom drawer, I tugged out three thick leather-bound books, one with a red cover and two with black. The red book contained sales entries for the quarter thus far, inked in bright violet. "Oh...can we paint my room that color?" Twilight asked. "Wait, do I have a room?"

"Umm...I guess? Let's figure that out when the police let us inside." I looked down at the book. Several columns tracked whether an order was custom, the customer name, the product category, and a few other things. As expected, Denise didn't have a lot of transactions, but when she made a custom sale for fancy magical paper goods, she earned quite a bit at one time. Still, it didn't seem like much overall. But what did I know? I didn't know how much it cost to survive in the magical world.

I opened the first black book. It looked like a ledger with perfectly inked rows in red and black.

"That ink is so boring," Twilight declared.

I ignored her. I assumed each line tracked amounts paid and owed, as the red and black lines balanced each other perfectly. But for what? The entries had one of two marks next to them: BTLY or DSKT. Maybe they referred to money she owed and paid her suppliers? I voiced my theory aloud to the business-savvy cat.

"You think she only had two suppliers? For all the paper and cardstock? The ink, ribbons, the ready-made journals, the—"

"Okay, you're right, Twilight." I moved on to the final book, which looked like an additional sales ledger. Unlike the red book, this one had been written in pale gray ink I could barely read. Twilight didn't even deign to comment on it. This one had fewer columns. One for price and two with codes. "Weird."

I moved on to the filing cabinets, which held past records as well as inventory and supplier records, so I

guess Twilight was right about Denise having many suppliers. I ran to the storeroom to ask Shea if I could borrow
her phone to take photos. My phone had died, and I had no
plans to charge it anytime soon. Phone in hand, I zoomed
back to snap photos of all three books in Denise's desk.

"Don't know why you're bothering," Twilight said when
I had the phone held over the book with gray ink.

"We might need them later."

For good measure, I shot a sample of the records in
the filing cabinet too. As the last drawer clicked shut,
Twilight's fur stood on end and Tansy zoomed into the
room. "The fuzz are here. Let's boogie."

I guess in a high-pressure situation, Tansy regressed
to slang from her death decade. Blessing my new pillowy
boots, I followed the ghost toward the storeroom, but Shea
walked right through Tansy as she rushed out, leaning
heavily on her cane. "We can't take the stairs. Peony Wilder
is talking to Martin Minor behind her shop. If they see
us..."

Tansy groaned. "Everyone will know within the hour."

I grabbed Shea's shoulders. "Can you shift and fly out
the back door without them seeing you?"

"Yes, but I *do not* abandon my friends."

I raised a brow. "You don't even know me. I could be a
killer. Now, go. I'll figure this out. The longer you argue,
the longer you delay me."

"Just go, Shea!" Tansy said.

"Ugh, fine."

As she stomped to the back door, I swiveled to Tansy. "Keep an eye out."

I ran back to Denise's office. *Page? Can you hear me?*

Yes. Remember, you own the building.

Sure, but it could look like I'm covering my murderous tracks. Do you have control over this space like you do the bookshop?

I felt his sigh, like book covers flapping in my mind. *Unfortunately not. My magic reach extends to the ceiling and no farther as to not unsettle tenants.*

The ceiling. I could work with that.

"Detective Fores is talking to Sylvie on the sidewalk, and a couple officers are hanging off to the side," Tansy called.

"Want me to go down there?" Twilight asked. "I could sneak out down the fire escape, run around front, and attack! Shred their clothes!"

"You have a bit of a violent streak, Twilight, and I don't hate it, but hold that thought." I threw open the window in Denise's office. I spotted two people talking behind the last shop in this stretch of the alley, on the other side of Pegasus Potions. They'd definitely see me emerge at street level, but maybe...

Page, there's a little window at the very top of the second floor. It's only about ten feet below me and a little to my right. Can you—

A heartbeat later, the window silently shot open, a platform of books formed just under the window, and a *slide* of more books floated up as high as Page's magic reached. I just had to jump.

Before I could tuck my feet up, Twilight sailed out the window. "Yippee! This is the best day of my life!"

With much less glee, I swung my legs out and pushed off the windowsill. My knees hit the books first, and the hardbacks tilted me up so I slid through the window feet first.

I converted my scream to a squeak so as not to draw attention, but the fall I expected never came. Page caught me on a bed of kids' books, where Twilight awaited me. We sailed across the second floor to the forested section as if on a magic carpet. A raven flew in behind us and squawked at our side.

When Page set us down, I stayed huddled on the books. Twilight leaped onto my lap. Shea shifted back to human, still holding her cane. Shifter magic was pretty cool. They took everything with them in the instant they shifted, including mobility devices, apparently.

Tansy floated down. "Detective Fores and the officers just went up to search and ward the property." She smiled. "Good thinking to go this morning, Kinley. Once the ward raises, no way would you get in there. The detective's wards are rock solid."

I nodded. "I've known Ryland for less than a day, and I'd be surprised if anything he did was less than rock solid."

"His jawline is rock solid," Shea said.

Tucking my hair behind my ears, I said, "Oh? I hadn't noticed."

She tapped her cane. "Mm hmm. Sure. So, did anyone find anything? Nothing in the storeroom seemed odd to me. She had supplies, a few orders in progress, and a couple completed orders. All normal."

Tansy shrugged. "Everything seemed fine in the front. None of the magic had been disturbed. I did get a kick out of a card that will break up with the recipient via a vulgar gesture."

Twilight rolled around on her back, laughing and getting fur all over my pants.

"I'm not sure if we found anything helpful." I explained the records we'd reviewed. "Most of it seemed normal, though something seemed a bit off. I don't know what, but I took pictures."

"Good," Tansy said. "Well, I hate to do this, but the planning committee for the Halloween festival meets today, so I need to get going."

"Ghosts serve on committees?"

"Kinley! That's so rude," Twilight said, her laughter finally breaking.

Tansy didn't seem offended. "Yes. I need something to fill my eternal afterlife. Event planning suits me."

"She's the head of the committee," Shea said. "Since she took over, tourism has increased threefold during the festival. Probably because she doesn't need sleep!" She leaned over from the edge of my book carpet to pat Twilight on the head. "I have to go too. Animals don't know it's Sunday, and I run the animal shelter."

Twilight perked up. "Can I come see the dogs?"

"You can go see the dogs another time," I said. "Thanks for your help today, Tansy and Shea."

"I'm just so happy you're home." Tansy wiped at her glistening eyes.

"Do you want to catch up tonight?" Shea asked. "We could grab a drink at The Seer's Stout."

"Oh!" Years had passed since a potential friend had invited me for a drink. I'd have typically made an excuse, but I actually *wanted* to go. "I'd like that, but I can't. Can we go another night? My neighbors made me promise to have dinner with them and their niece."

"Miguel, Uncle Moonbite, and Zori? I'm *so* there. Z and I are good friends, and her uncles *love* me, of course. I'll bring bread, because you can never have enough bread."

Uncle Moonbite? *Moon*? Please tell me they don't have werewolves on this island. I decided to focus on the bread. "I couldn't agree more. Bread comes first. Always. I hadn't thought about bringing anything..."

"Umm, you're bringing *me*." Twilight said.

"Oh, don't go out of your way." Tansy brushed her hand just above my arm. "They'd never want you to worry. Bring yourself and Twilight."

My familiar rubbed her face on my thigh. "See? I'm all you need."

Chapter Ten

"**D**on't worry, Twilight, we have some shredded chicken for you and Dawn," Miguel said as he placed an overflowing tray of veggie lasagna on the long dining table made from ocean driftwood.

Saliva practically spilled from my mouth as I breathed in the savory scents of garlic, basil, cheese, and tomato and the yeasty aroma of Shea's three types of bread. It had been too long since I'd had a sandwich with Sylvie at noon up in Page's forest. When she'd heard about Denise, she'd come by with food and a box of headache potions. We'd talked for a couple hours before she needed to get back to work.

"Of course, we have some bamboo for Sunset too," Sundar added, coming in with serving utensils and plates.

Zori's red panda familiar nestled inside Dawn's tail on a giant dog bed, but his ears perked at the mention of bamboo.

"I wasn't worried," Twilight said. "I'm just so grateful to be here." I repeated her words to everyone. She curled up next to the red panda. I couldn't help but smile at how quickly Twilight had made friends with Dawn and Sunset.

"Wait." I looked around the table. "Are all familiars named after times of day? I've met Midnight, Dusk, Dawn, Sunset, and Twilight."

Shea laughed from the seat to my left, the sound echoing off the steel-blue walls of the dining room. "Remember Carl? Tansy's ghost familiar."

"They'd run out of names quickly if all familiars had times-of-day names," Azura, a tall, Black fairy I'd met a few minutes earlier, said. She sat on my right, smiling at me with perfectly blushed deep-brown cheeks and mauve-painted lips. The chair she'd modified with a snap of her fingers now accommodated her tall golden wings while still supporting her back.

When Shea invited herself tonight, she dragged Azura along too, as they were both good friends of Zori's. The witch, shifter, and fairy had an easy rapport full of laughter and affection that somehow both put me at ease and made me uncomfortable.

I'd never had friends who expressed such tenderness before, and the way they so easily anticipated each other's needs amazed me. Shea tipping the smallest bit of wine into Azura's glass while filling Zori's nearly to the brim.

Azura cutting Shea off a hulking piece of bread. Zori taking care not to touch Azura's curtain of gold-dusted black box braids when she brushed a piece of fluff off her friend's blouse.

"It is odd about the familiars, though," Azura said. "Five with names related to the diurnal cycle."

Zori reached for a carafe of water, almost knocking over a bottle of wine. Azura snapped her fingers, and the bottle stabilized. Zori barely noticed, like this happened twelve times an hour. "I know Dusk, but who is Midnight?"

I perked up. "Midnight is Ryland's familiar and the cutest little thing I've ever seen, with his puffs of steam and tiny dragon wings." Twilight cleared her throat. "Cutest thing other than you," I shot over my shoulder at the pile of familiars. Twilight's sweet little face, soft gray coat, and penchant for hopping up and down on her feet *were* adorable.

"You've got a moon bear shifter for a neighbor too," Sundar said with a cheesy knife pointed at himself. He resumed cutting the lasagna. "That's kinda similar."

Oh, wands and willows. The Uncle Moonbite nickname made more sense now. No werewolves! Just moon bears.

I'd only seen moon bears online, and they were cute as heck, but I doubted Sundar wanted to shift at the table just so I could admire his black fur with the signature white V on the chest.

Setting bowls down for the familiars, Miguel said, "You must have some odd celestial affinity, Kinley. Twilight,

Midnight, a moon bear. You're drawing them in! If fairies had familiars, Azura, yours would have to be named Day."

She laughed, the sound like the rush of wings as a bird lifts off. "Who needs familiars when you have nature. No offense," she added to the eating creatures behind us, but only Sunset seemed to be listening as he chomped on a length of bamboo. He ambled over on two legs and smacked her leg with it, but his eyes held no reproach.

The husbands relied on Miguel's magic to lift and plate six pieces of lasagna without letting any bits slide out. I loved magic.

I focused on the best hexin' meal I'd had in ages, swishing delicious wine and taking massive bites of bread and cheesy zucchini-and-squash-filled lasagna.

"Kinley?" I looked up to find Sundar looking at me with an amused twinkle in his eye.

I swallowed my last bite. "Sorry, did you say something?"

"Would you like some merlot?"

Using one finger, I pushed forward my empty glass. "Yes, please. That pinot noir made me want to die."

He laughed. "That's what I like to hear. I own Wishing Well Wines, a wine bar and store down the street from The Perfect Page."

"Well, you've made a customer out of me tonight."

"How's Page?" Zori asked, twirling her hair. "I love sitting in there on my days off."

As I leaned back in my chair, I wasn't sure if the wine or the genuine interest on the five faces around me loosened my tongue, but I told them all about bonding with Page.

"Page became a part of me. It felt *weird*. Ever since the Huberts, my first foster family, died not long after I turned nine, I haven't felt any kind of familial connection. I like it, but I don't know what to do with it."

"Enjoy it! All of it," Shea said, smacking the table. "Page, Twilight, magic, Sea Sprite." She snagged her elbow around my neck. "Reconnecting with me. Meeting these fine folks."

With my cheeks smooshed between her forearm and bicep, I said, "I'm twying."

She released me. "You had fun this morning. I saw you looking at that forest, then you got to fly through a window!"

Zori clapped her hands, almost sending her wine glass spinning down the table. "You flew?"

Azura leaned in, her pointed ears twitching and mahogany eyes shining. "You went into the forest?"

"Definitely not, Zori, and I want to hear about this forest later, Azura." I told them all about Page's new forest theme and how he'd helped me escape Denise's shop that afternoon.

Miguel wriggled his wand around, sending the plates to the kitchen. "Wow, I didn't know Page had that depth of magic."

"I feel, literally," I said, rubbing my sternum, "that Page has more magic than we could ever understand."

"If only he could magic up Denise's murderer for you, Kin," Shea said.

Azura's wings wiggled, and she ran her finger down her jawline. "Gossip might help in this situation."

Shea grabbed her chest, and Zori gulped in a melodramatic gasp.

Miguel laughed and jostled his niece's shoulder. "Stop it, you." He looked at me. "Azura isn't big on gossip."

Azura shrugged. "*Pointless* gossip bores me, but this has a point. I'm not saying Kinley should go around town asking everyone about Denise. She should go to Pixie Dust. Denise went there every night without fail. You know Tabitha on the night shift adores gossiping. She said something to me about Denise's trash—the trash at her house, maybe?—but I tuned her out. Tabitha will surely have no problem spilling the mugwort to you about it, Kinley."

I set a hand on Azura's shoulder. "I don't usually gossip much either, so I'm on your side there." Azura fluttered her fingers in her braids, wisps of gold dust creating a halo around her as she flashed triumphant eyes at her friends.

"If Tabitha might have info on Denise and her, umm, trash, I'm all for chatting," I continued. "What's Pixie Dust, and where do I find it?"

"The bakery," Sundar said. "Azura brought a cinnamon torte from Pixie Dust. Let me get it."

With that, we moved onto dessert while Azura told me all about the beautiful forest that took up half the island. With humans having no access to Sea Sprite Isle, the woods had come alive with many species of magical plants and animals. "I'll take you," she said, as if folding me under her wing and into her life was as easy as those three words. "You can stop by my work someday, and we'll go into the forest."

"Where do you work?"

"My family owns a hotel, but it's very nature-oriented. It's right where the forest meets the ocean, not far from Foxglove Point. We think of it more like an experience than a hotel."

"Wow, I'd love to see it."

"We can fly there!" A piece of torte flung off Zori's fork, and Dawn quickly snagged it.

I stopped chewing and just stared at Zori. "You want me to get on a one inch thick chunk of wood?"

Zori tucked her waves behind her ears, growing serious. "I'll teach you. I'm an air witch and a flying instructor. Part time, though I hope to make it full time soon. If I spill one more drink at Mystic Mugs, it might have to be *really* soon."

I raised a brow at Shea.

"Don't worry. She's only clumsy on the ground. In the air, she's more graceful than I am."

Zori could out-fly an actual bird shifter? It didn't matter. "I'm not getting on a broom. Nope. I've done a lot in the last twenty-eight hours, but I am not flying."

"We'll see about that," Zori muttered.

A sound like a lion battling a lawn mower made me jump almost high enough to fly. I turned around to find Twilight draped across Sunset, snoring. That answered whether she would get her own room. Looking out the window, I saw that both sunset and twilight had long passed, and midnight would arrive in only a few hours.

I offered to help clean up, but Sundar insisted on walking me home instead. Zori promised to come see me the next day and everyone pulled me into hugs, which I found myself enjoying. I scooped Twilight into my arms and let Uncle Moonbite walk me home with only his namesake to light our path.

Chapter Eleven

"So, how do I run a bookshop?" I asked, setting my decaf latte on the front counter of The Perfect Page.

Decaf not because I wanted to drag my boots all day, but because I'd woken with a migraine, and I'd found caffeine aggravated an existing migraine. Light had insisted on torturing me that morning, causing throbbing pain to invade my forehead, temples, jaw, and eyes. I'd stumbled to the bathroom, slightly off balance, to find my pupils tiny despite the dim light in the room. With my skin pale and clammy, I'd looked seconds away from joining Tansy on the other side.

Having already taken the maximum number of acute migraine pills for the month, I'd downed one of the headache potions Sylvie had given me the day before. It had only knocked things down to a level four on the pain scale.

"Are you sure you should learn this today, Kinley?" Twilight asked, the tip of her tail brushing against my hand on the counter.

I pushed my pink-lensed migraine glasses up my nose. "I'm fine. A level-four migraine won't stop me. What alternative do I have, anyway? Sit at home considering my impending arrest for Denise's murder?"

"That will not happen," Zori said, walking into the store with an armful of pastries, two of which she dropped. "Whoops." As she retrieved them, Sunset crawled off her shoulders, scaled a bookshelf, and closed his eyes.

I'd forgotten to lock the door behind me again, but the closed sign and lack of lighting would stop any would-be customers.

Zoriana is correct, Page rumbled, his voice rolling through my bones. *Denise's attitude made her many enemies. We will find the one that finally cracked.*

"Yeah! We'll find the killer." Twilight said, sniffing the pastries Zori placed on the counter.

I snagged a double-chocolate muffin and repeated Page and Twilight's words for Zori, adding, "Until we find the killer, I need to stay busy. Learning to run the bookshop would help."

"Or," Zori said with a devilish grin, "you could learn to fly."

"Thanks for the pastries, but no thanks on the flying lesson. How did you know I would be here? I'm glad you came, though."

She smiled, her sepia eyes shining. "My coworker at Mystic Mugs texted me that the 'lady from Hijinx who killed Denise' came in for coffee and went into the bookstore."

I tugged on the sleeves of my navy cable-knit sweater. Great. Even if Ryland didn't arrest me, everyone would think the new, unhinged witch killed Denise. "I forgot about that teenager who filmed me and Denise arguing. Hijinx is some kind of magical social media?"

Zori nodded. "Yep. We have CharmChat too, but all the teens use Hijinx, where they can 'Hijinx their hijinks.'" She pulled her phone out. "If you give me your number, I can just text you next time."

I rattled off the numbers. "My phone died on Saturday. I haven't charged it." The ache in my eyes increased as I thought about potential texts asking about my breakup with Aaron.

Their opinions do not matter. That worm did not deserve you.

I smiled. *Thanks, Page.*

Zori tucked her phone away. "Going off grid. I like it. So, we're learning to run a bookshop?"

Thirty minutes later, I regretted my decision. "Okay, I get that the magical register makes certain things easier, like ringing up an entire book stack at once, but the cash system is way too complicated."

You're overthinking it, Page said.

"You're overthinking it," Zori said.

"I've never over-thought anything in my life."

Twilight giggled. "You stared into your grandma's closet for fifteen minutes this morning before you pulled out that sweater."

I rounded on her. "It isn't easy pulling clothes from the wardrobe of someone almost fifty years your senior and much shorter than you. And as I reminded you several times, not everyone has fancy computer software to model all their clothes like Cher in *Clueless*."

The cat just rolled on her back. "Whatever, I'm sure there's magic for that."

Page's sigh rumbled through me. *Let's focus.*

I turned back to the register. "Fine." I tapped the touch screen to activate it. What was I supposed to say? "Umm...EJECT for a manual count to—Ahh!" I jumped back as the register drawer shot open and a spray of one-dollar bills hit me in the face.

All three of my companions lost it, their laughter taking the edge off my annoyance. My lips curved up, but I caught Tansy sweeping into the store faster than a witch on a broom.

She passed through the counter and halted, her eyes huge. "Okay, play along. Denise is *here*. In the break room, okay? This shady kid was trying to look through the ward upstairs. He said he really needed to find Denise, so—"

The door opened and a wiry white guy in jeans and a long sleeve T-shirt stepped into the shop. He couldn't be over twenty, but the dark circles under his eyes and shifty glances around the shop aged him. He slipped his thumbs into two belt loops before pulling them out and tucking his hands into his pockets.

"Can I help you?" I asked as I picked up the bills and closed the register.

He flitted his eyes to Tansy. "I need to see Denise."

"She's in the break room, right?" Tansy asked me, pointing toward the door to the back.

My brow furrowed. What did she think would happen when we got to the small kitchen that sat next to the office inside the storeroom?

Zori twirled a lock of her hair and leaned over the counter. "Why do you need Denise? She wanted some quiet time."

"She'll want to see me. Trust me." He looked up. "We have a standing appointment."

Tansy and I exchanged a look. Why would this kid need a standing appointment with a stationery store owner?

"This kid reeks of anxiety," Twilight told me.

Zori smiled at him. "Oh, she must have forgotten to call you. Her shop needs repairs. That's why it has a ward—for safety. She's not taking customers right now. Do you need a journal? We sell some here."

"What? No, I'm not here to buy anything." He winced as he realized what he'd admitted. "I need to get back to Meadowsweet soon, so I'd appreciate it if you'd get Denise."

I mouthed "Meadowsweet" at Zori.

"It's another magical town in California," she whispered.

This shifter is involved in something nefarious, Page informed me.

How do you know?

I can read each magical being's energy to know if they're a witch, fairy, or shifter.

No, how do you know he's involved in something nefarious?

Ah, because he needs these books.

Two paperbacks whizzed toward me, stopping beneath the counter so the kid couldn't see them.

How to Reform Your Criminal Ways

How to End Unwanted Relationships

Tansy and Zori read the titles too. We exchanged glances.

The kid ran a hand through his sandy-blond hair. "I *really* need to speak with Denise."

My heel squeaked as I turned. "Okay. Let's go."

I looked up. *Your creativity would be helpful here, Page.*

Somehow, he winked at me in my mind.

I led the way to the small kitchen, zigzagging through the inventory of books in the stockroom until we reached the open door. Stepping aside, I said, "After you."

A short counter with cherry cabinets underneath could be seen from outside the kitchen, but he didn't spot the empty square table with four chairs until he stepped inside. We pushed in behind him.

Turning, he said, "Is Denise in the bath—" He jumped six inches back when he noticed the door had disappeared.

"Hey! That's not cool." The kid looked at my and Zori's hands, as if expecting to see wands held aloft. "Where's the door? Where's Denise?"

A chair at the table moved itself out.

"You might want to sit down for this news," Tansy said.

He crossed his arms. "Umm, no?"

The chair flew across the room and hit the back of his knees. He stumbled backward into it.

"Okay, Page, I think we've terrorized him enough." I muttered.

A grumble like the fluttering of pages was his only reply.

"As if," Twilight said from next to my feet. "Let's terrorize him more."

Ignoring her, I said, "I'm sorry. Page, the bookshop, got a little enthusiastic. I hate to do this, but we need answers."

"Well, so do I. Where. Is. Denise?"

My teeth caught my lip. I didn't know their relationship, so how should I tell—

"She's dead," Zori said.

Like that, apparently.

Shock followed by intense relief passed over his features.

The kid tried to hide it with the worst impression of mourning I'd ever seen. "I'm sorry to hear that. She was a, err, nice lady."

Zori laughed. "Sure. You two were clearly best buds."

Tansy glided forward and crouched in front of him. "There's more. Someone murdered Denise. We need to find the killer."

He ran a hand down his thin face. "I'm not surprised, if I'm honest, but this has nothing to do with me. Can you bring the door back?"

I grabbed one of the other chairs, set it next to him, and sat down. With my legs crossed and my chin resting in my hand, I said, "No. We need to know the nature of your relationship with Denise."

His jaw ticked. "Not happening. You can't keep me here. It's illegal."

I let my eyes focus on him for too long. Waited for him to shift uncomfortably. "True. Shall we call the police? I'm sure they'd also be interested in how you knew her."

He sucked in a breath, but stayed quiet.

"I've got all day." I said.

"Me too," Tansy said.

Zori looked at her watch. "I've actually got a lesson to teach at—"

Tansy silenced her with a glance, and Zori leaned against the wall.

"What's your name?" I asked. "I'm Kinley. This is Tansy, Zori, and Twilight."

He squirmed in his chair, like a rodent caught by its tail, but after a few moments, he sighed. "Tyler."

"Thank you. Tyler, you obviously didn't kill Denise. You wouldn't have come looking for her if you had. But something shady is going on, and we need to know what. I promise, we won't judge you."

Zori caught my eye and mouthed, "Show him the books."

Page, can you send in the books?

The two paperbacks flew through the wall, and I held them out for Tyler. "Page always knows what books you need. These books show you want to be done with this situation. Everything you say will remain confidential. If you don't help us, an innocent person might go to prison for Denise's murder."

He stared at the books, and for a second, I thought he'd cry, but he settled on rubbing his hands over his face and through his hair. "Fine. I'll tell you." Tyler blew out a breath and mussed his hair again. "Three semesters ago, I needed cash. Badly. I started...assisting other students at my college with their work. The money was fine, but they wanted a way to get around the anti-cheating spells on exams. A *contact* told me about Denise."

Tansy tugged on her bowler hat. "I take it Denise didn't just sell stationery and invitations."

He shook his head. "She had a side business providing other, uh, services."

I pinched my chin between two fingers. "She helped you cheat on exams?"

"Yep. We came up with a system. I'm a ferret shifter, so it's easy for me to get into professors' offices unseen. I also have an eidetic memory, so I could recall everything I saw on upcoming exam papers. If the answers weren't there, I'd prepare them. Denise would take the information from me and load it into special pens."

Tyler's eyes relaxed a smidge. "As much as I hated Denise, she had talent. The pens carried a spell to release the answers only when you tapped on each question. For something short answer or math based, the ink would appear in a light gray, almost invisible ink so you could rewrite it in your own words and handwriting."

Zori let out a low whistle. "That's impressive magic. So detailed. I'm guessing the anti-cheating spells didn't activate because most cheating spells enhance the caster's performance. They don't use a physical object to provide answers."

"Exactly." Tyler squirmed again as he looked at the frown on Tansy's face. "Look, I know it was wrong. I only wanted to do it a few times. Denise had other ideas. When I came for the last pens I'd planned to buy, she threatened me. Not only that, she raised her fee. A lot."

Twilight's ears flattened. "That's so not cool! You should have shifted and bitten her ankles until she bled."

Such a violent kitty. I did not translate her words.

Tansy's brow unfurled. "Sorry, Tyler. I didn't mean to look judgmental. I'm sorry Denise threatened you."

Tyler huffed. "Me too. Denise said she'd turn me into the university. Said she had proof of our partnership. Said I had to continue selling exam answers and pay her more, which left me almost nothing." His fingers clenched. "She told me I had to keep doing it after I finished school too. She could turn me in even years after I graduated and the school could revoke my degree. I had no choice but to keep going until she let me stop."

This poor kid. He'd done something wrong, but he'd wanted to stop. Denise had backed him into a corner. No wonder he'd looked so relieved about her death. Could there have been others out there just as relieved?

"It's over now," I said. "Someone made sure of that. Do you have any idea what other services she provided or to whom?"

"No. Just that she used ink and paper. I got the impression she could do a lot more than cheat on exams. Dangerous things." The chair creaked as he suddenly straightened. "Hexes. One of her customers could have killed her. This whole thing's going to break open, isn't it? The police will figure it out." Tyler's breathing quickened. "They'll look at her customers. What if they think *I* killed her?"

Zori crossed to him and put a hand on his shoulder. "Hey, it's okay. Take a breath. I'll do it too." They each pulled in a long stream of air. "Maybe you have an alibi. Denise died Saturday night or early Sunday morning."

Tyler snapped his fingers. "Yes! I was at a lock-in on campus for charity. We were magically sealed inside a large gymnasium."

"Do you have proof?" I asked, my public relations brain kicking in. "Witnesses are good, but what about photos?"

He slid his phone out and pulled up CharmChat. A few seconds later, Tyler showed me a post tagging @bigtylerlovesyou. I scrolled through ten photos of him eating tacos, drinking beer, playing carnival games, and standing near a board tracking donations. "Good. This should really help you."

"The portal won't have a record of you coming through either," Tansy added. "There are other ways to get to the island, but you couldn't sneak away from your lock-in and back on the same night without using the portal that connects Meadowsweet and Sea Sprite."

Zori gave him one more squeeze and stepped back. "You weren't doing anything illegal either. Cheating might be immoral, but you won't go to jail."

"Yeah, but if the police tell my school..." he trailed off before standing. "Can I leave now?" The door reappeared, and he stood. "Denise sucked, but I hope you find the killer so that no one innocent goes down for her death."

So did I. This felt like a breakthrough. Denise had a shady side hustle and had no qualms about blackmail. This was certainly better than knowing she sneered at her neighbors about fallen leaves. Though, I shouldn't disregard any town gossip, no matter how small.

Reminded of gossip, I looked at Tansy and Zori. "What time does the night shift start at the bakery? I need to find Tabitha."

Chapter Twelve

Pixie Dust sat next to The Starlit Broomstick on Toil Avenue. I refused to even look inside the broomstick store, instead keeping my eyes on the purple-dusted white sign that told me I'd arrived at the bakery.

After over thirty years alive, one expects certain things upon walking into a bakery, but when I pulled open Pixie Dust's glass door, shielding my eyes from the afternoon glare, those expectations shattered.

Had I entered a business or a meadow? A bakery or a florist?

A cacophony of flowers sprouted from the walls and ceiling, gold dust dripping like pollen from the purple, pink, and white flowers hanging above.

Twilight and I stopped, letting the dust gather on our clothes and fur, watching it disappear moments later. It reminded me of the dust on Azura's hair the night before.

I tore my eyes away to inspect the purple tables, which had shoots of lavender growing from their centers. Even the black hexagonal floor tiles had a golden sheen, like the pixie dust had been set into the stone.

A bird call behind us announced another customer entering. We stepped aside to let them approach the long black counter with a glass pastry case atop it. I watched as the flowers rooted along the front panel of the counter writhed, showing off for their new guest.

As if worried I might be jealous, a thin vine extended from the ceiling and brushed the crown of my head.

"Oh, me too!" Twilight said, dancing in place on her paws. I scooped her up and raised my arms so the vine could brush my familiar's ears. Twilight shivered.

"It's special, huh?" a confident voice called.

I looked to the counter where a tall white fairy with fluttering tangerine wings stood, her bushel of blond curls pulled back, the spirals bursting above the clip like a bouquet. "You look like a first timer," she said.

Still holding Twilight, I approached her. "You caught me. Whoa." My eyes roamed over the wall behind the fairy. A meadow. Not a painting. A real meadow you could step into, complete with shining sun and swaying flowers. "Is that a portal?"

The woman chuckled. "No, it's just really good magic."

The bird call behind me sounded again. I glanced over my shoulder at two young men stepping into line. The taller one elbowed the other, and they began whispering while looking at me.

"Maybe they don't like the sweater you spent all morning picking out," Twilight said.

A sharp snap of fingers drew my attention back to the Pixie Dust employee. "Oh, I knew you looked familiar. You're the new Paigewright. The one they're saying killed Denise. It's all over CharmChat."

Her amber eyes had transformed, a conspiratorial gleam shining, begging me for my side of the story. I flicked my eyes to the name embroidered on her black apron: Tabitha. Exactly who Azura had told me to find.

I leaned against the bakery case, looking left and right before whispering, "I didn't kill her, but someone wants me to take the fall."

Tabitha's wings went from a flutter to a hum to rival a hummingbird. "Do you know who? Or why? Denise was so mean and grumpy. She came here every night. No one liked her. No. One. I'm not surprised someone killed her."

With my lip between my teeth, like I was trying to stop myself, I said, "That's what I've heard too. I don't know who killed her, but I found out she had *enemies*." You had to give something to get something when it came to rumors.

Tabitha let out a delighted squeak. She was a thick sponge that could never be soaked with enough gossip. "Who?"

"I don't know. I'm trying to find out."

The young men moved up to the counter to place their order with another employee. I ignored their gawking.

"You said Denise came here every night? Did you ever see her with anyone?"

Tabitha snorted. "She came alone at eight p.m. She ordered tea and our cookie of the day while acting superior as all hex, sat at the same table, and complained about at least one thing before leaving."

I rolled my eyes. "Denise and I met *once*, and that sounds right to me."

"Ugh, I'd have dipped my tail in her tea," Twilight said.

I held back a chuckle.

Tabitha slapped her hands on top of the glass and continued. "Only one time did someone else show up—her *husband*. Just a few months ago."

I wrinkled my nose. "Her ex-husband?"

"No, that's the thing. Everyone thinks they're divorced, but it never went through. Denise made it so difficult that he gave up. It's hard not to hear customer conversations at that time of night. It's not long before we close, and it's empty in here. He went on about how he didn't want to try anymore. How she'd drawn things out for years. How he didn't need a piece of paper to formalize their separation. How Denise could keep the money. He said he just wanted to be with his girlfriend."

Twilight's tail swished across my face. "Interesting. That sounds like a motive. He could have made that big scene to make people think he didn't care about the divorce or the money."

Very true.

"Wow. Maybe I'll add him to my list of potential enemies, though I don't think he's at the same *level* as the others."

Tabitha's wings went into overtime, and she practically lifted off the ground. "You must know something about these enemies."

"Oh my cauldrons, Kinley, she is eating this up," Twilight said. "Keep going. Make her think it has something to do with trash. Remember, Azura told us Tabitha talked about Denise's trash?"

My voice dropped to a hint of a whisper. "Denise's trash may have had something to do with it."

"Holy spell! I *knew* it. Denise lived near here. She'd walk over, but she didn't come straight inside. She'd pause as she passed the alley around back. Always waiting until no one was around, she'd sneak up to the dumpster. Her black tote bag would have a little plastic grocery bag tucked inside that she'd toss out. None of us would have noticed if not for our employee, Ivan, who has X-ray vision and saw her through the back wall. He started watching for her. She did it every night."

"So. Shady," Twilight said.

Denise clearly had something she didn't want in her home or office. Waste from her side hustle, perhaps?

"You don't happen to know what she had in the grocery bag, do you?"

Tabitha shook her head. "I tried to look one night. When I took out the trash, I ran into her in the alley. Literally.

Denise got the tiniest bit of icing on her. Before I could apologize, she screamed at me, called me incompetent, etcetera."

She pulled her strong shoulders back. "I'd had enough after that. I finally just asked Denise why she threw her trash in our dumpster every night. She just yelled some more. I decided to look in the bag after she left. It was a huge privacy violation, but I figured she'd lost that privilege by being a banshee. When I pulled the bag out, I saw Madam Malfina walking by the mouth of the alley and giving me a funny look. Seers kinda creep me out, so I dropped it and fled inside."

Tabitha sighed. "I swear, that whole street is weird. There's Papa Gunther, who makes everyone call him Papa. There's Mrs. Briarwood who orders a cake for herself every Saturday—that one's not weird, more like life goals—and there's Lisa, who thinks mushrooms can cure literally any ailment ever and talks about it constantly."

Okay, I could understand why Azura tuned out Tabitha. I didn't care about any of that. "So, you didn't get to see inside the bag."

"Nope."

I sighed. "Frick. When did that happen?"

Tabitha shrugged. "About a year and a half ago. I remember it was the day of the Lights of Love festival."

"Thanks. Anything else about Denise?"

"No." She tapped her hands. "Do *you* know anything else?"

Did I know anything innocuous I could tell her? The more I shared, the more she'd want to tell me anything new she might learn. "Do you know about Denise's wrist?"

Her pupils widened, ready to soak up my juicy gossip. I filled her in while I ordered a lavender blueberry scone, two—okay, three—chocolate chip cookies, and a familiar-safe mini strawberry muffin. Twilight wove around my feet as Tabitha slipped the goodies into a purple bag.

Tucking it inside my tote, I started to turn. "Let me know if you hear anything else about Deni—oof."

My glasses squashed against my face as I slammed into a human wall. I looked up. Scratch that. A witch wall.

Ryland grabbed my shoulders to steady me before he guided us away from the counter. "You okay?"

I really needed to stop ending up on this guy's chest.

"Ooooh, the detective!" Twilight sniffed his sneakers—again the same shoes, but in a banana yellow today. "You know, he really is cute, Kinley. Should we do a makeover so you can go on a date with him, like in *Clueless*?"

My new boot may have *accidentally* kicked out and *accidentally* scooted her across the floor into a koala bear sleeping under a table, who was either very lost or someone's familiar.

"Yeah, I'm fine," I said, my voice an octave too high. "Sorry to smash into you! Are you here for a baked good? I mean, this is a bakery, so, of course you are. Isn't it pretty in here? This is my first time inside." A vine came down from the ceiling to caress my reddening cheeks, and I fell silent.

Ryland's lips twitched. "I'm not here for a baked good. I came for you."

Midnight poked his head out of Ryland's black jacket, helpfully distracting me from the warmth in my chest. "Hi, Midnight. Why did you and Ryland come to see me?"

The detective tickled Midnight's chin with a finger. "Midnight says he came because he wants to know if you'll be his friend. I came because my MBI boss wants me to interrogate you."

I continued addressing the dragon. "Of course I will be your friend. Now, as your friend, can I ask you to blow some smoke at your witch? Because I do not need to be interrogated today."

Ryland held his hands up just as Midnight let out a tiny "RAWR!" with a puff of steam. "Hang on. I'm not going to interrogate you. I told him I'd do an informal questioning, but I had something else in mind."

I crossed my arms. "What's that?"

The tips of his slightly lopsided ears went slightly pink—nowhere near as red as my cheeks had just been. "I thought you might like to get some things from your place in Portland."

All my bluster fell away. "Oh. Ryland, I appreciate that." I gestured to my comfy yet too short pants. "It would be nice to have pants that meet the tops of my boots."

"Then let's go outside, and I'll open a portal."

"One second."

Twilight and the koala had formed one sleepy lump of gray fur under the table. I extracted her, one paw at a time, with Ryland crouched at my side. "How did you find me here?" I asked.

"Ah, someone posted an image of you talking to Tabitha on CharmChat. I have an alert for tags related to you and Denise in case anything relevant comes up."

"You mean in case someone comments their name, number, and address with a full confession?"

Ryland laughed. "You never know."

Tucking my snoring cat close, I stood. As we walked to the door, I glared at the two guys who'd whispered about me, sure they'd been the ones to post my photo.

We stepped onto the brick sidewalk, and the detective said, "You ready? Once you decide what you want to take today, I can open as wide a portal from your condo to your house as we need and float stuff through."

I cringed, suddenly unsure about this. But I really needed a few things. With my head bent into Twilight's fur, I said, "You'll only need to make it a normal door width."

Ryland pretended not to notice my weird reaction and slashed open the portal. He took my arm, and a second later, we stood in my condo.

"Kinley...this is not what I expected."

Chapter Thirteen

My stomach clenched, and I waited for a wave of judgment, but Ryland turned to me with a huge smile.

"The view! Kinley, wow." He walked up to the floor-to-ceiling windows of my condo's living room and practically plastered his face to the glass. I relaxed as he gaped at the city of Portland like a kid at the zoo. "The city, the river. Amazing." Midnight climbed out of his pocket and flew up to his shoulder, looking at the city with wide eyes.

Twilight joined them. "I agree. This is ah-maz-ing."

I shielded my eyes, wanting to close the curtains, but hesitant to take the view away from them. "It's why I bought this place. I love sitting here in the mornings with my coffee and at night with my tea." The city felt like a friend—one of the only constants in the ever-changing landscape of my childhood. So, when I didn't have a migraine, I'd open the tall curtains and greet it each morning and say goodnight after my last drop of tea.

Twilight turned around. "Where's all your stuff?"

I tensed again.

She jumped onto my gray sectional and sat on the one white chenille blanket. "Everything's bare. The walls, the coffee table, the TV stand. Except for the bookshelf. Did you just move in?"

"No, it's been five years."

Ryland turned around, and I gestured at my familiar. "She asked how long I've been here."

He saw me wincing, pulled out his wand, and whisked the curtains closed except for a sliver of light. Then Ryland's eyes roamed over the few pieces of furniture, noticing the same things Twilight had—until he saw the kitchen at the other end of the open space. "*Nice*. You could really cook in here," he said, rushing past the island to the far wall and opening the fridge. He turned horrified eyes on me.

I couldn't help but laugh as I followed him. "I know. A few condiments, a takeout container from Thursday night, and some random sandwich ingredients."

"Half of which need to go in the trash immediately, Kin." Ryland tilted his head. "Can I call you Kin?"

I mirrored him. "Can I call you Ry?"

His lips twitched. "Only my friends call me Ry."

"Am I not your friend?"

"I don't usually tackle my friends on their wedding day, Kin."

"Sounds like your friends are boring, Ry."

Twilight skidded into the room. "Twi rhymes with Ry! Oh, and Midnight can go by Nigh."

I looked at Ryland, making my voice serious. "Twilight would like to start a name club with Ry, Twi, and Nigh." I reached forward to tickle the dragon's chin. "That's you, buddy." He meeped and flapped his wings.

"And you?" Ryland asked, eyes shining.

"I don't believe I'm included."

He chuckled and turned into the kitchen. "You don't use this room, do you?"

I shrugged, leaning on the island. "The toaster, the coffee pot, and the microwave have become good friends of mine."

He ran a hand down the counter. "As a kitchen witch, I can tell you this quartz feels unfulfilled just sitting here gathering toaster crumbs."

Twilight jumped onto the island. "You're a kitchen witch? Holy spell. Can you make me salmon tartare? Wait, you make portals and wards...*and* you're a kitchen witch?"

Huh? I repeated her words for him with a furrowed brow.

He ran a hand down the back of his head. "Yeah," he told her. "I know, it's rare. My mom and brother are both kitchen witches, way better than me, and I just happened to get a couple more primary powers too."

"Umm, what are you two talking about?" I asked.

My familiar sat up straight. "Witches have primary and secondary magics, Kinley. Your bibliomancy is a primary power. All witches have at least one such magic. Secondary magic is available to every witch. Cleaning the dishes, floating objects, things like that."

"So Zori's air magic is primary?" I asked.

"Yes, as are Ryland's portal, ward, and kitchen magics. Having three is quite rare."

Ryland's banana sneaker drew a line across the tile as I echoed her words for him. "It's no big deal."

Midnight gave Ryland a look and Twilight let out a little kitty snort. "One percent of witches have three primary magics. Thirteen percent have two."

"It sounds like a big deal, Ryland, but I'll pretend it's not if you forget about the state of my fridge."

He smiled. "Deal, but we aren't leaving until that all goes into the dumpster. Point me to the trash bags."

Despite my many protests, he insisted on cleaning out my fridge and just-as-bare pantry while Twilight and I packed.

"This shouldn't take long," I said to her as we entered the condo's sole bedroom.

Twilight jumped onto the white bed linens. "Because you don't have any stuff. Did you donate all your stuff like Cher did after the Pismo Beach disaster?"

My back stiffened. "You need to watch more movies than just *Clueless*. And who needs stuff? It's wasteful. Bad for the environment."

In truth, stuff was a liability. Stuff could be taken from you. Stuff weighed you down. I'd learned that when I'd had to pack a small bag to leave the Huberts and again and again as I moved from home to home as a kid.

She flicked her tail. "Right, the environment. Sure."

I grabbed my backpack to make sure my laptop was inside, then added the chargers from my nightstand. I opened the drawer and grabbed an eye massager that looked like a virtual reality headset, a heating mask for the eyes, and another heating pad for the jaw—all of which would have helped my migraine that morning. I already had my e-reader and phone in Sea Sprite, so I zipped the bag.

Dragging a large roller suitcase from the closet, I told Twilight to move or get crushed. She jumped out of the way but proceeded to lay in the suitcase once I'd opened it. I guess cats were cats, familiars or not.

Packing a bag to move on short notice felt as routine now as it had as a child. I swept my small pile of toiletries and makeup into a pouch and packed my hair tools so Page would stop commenting on my tresses.

But the closet gave me pause.

"Why are you just standing here?" Twilight asked, joining me.

I grazed my fingers over a soft row of suit jackets. "I think I hate all my clothes."

"Of course you do. Everything is drab. Have you heard of color?" She bounced on her toes. "We're definitely doing a makeover."

"You'd put me in all pink and yellow, so I'll pass, but you're right. These clothes...suck."

Black, navy, and gray blazers and slacks with the occasional pop of burgundy. Chinos, button downs, and Aaron-approved sweaters for the weekend, the combined effect of which made me look ready to step on a fancy boat at any second. Why had I let a man have a say in my weekend attire? How had I gotten so desperate for such a tiny sense of belonging that I'd given up such a large part of myself?

"You know what? I don't need any of this except..." I turned to grab three hangers that held fitted dark and black jeans I wore after work sometimes. I went back to the bedroom and tossed them into the case, then grabbed my puffy winter coat and a black softshell jacket. After adding my undergarments, soft pajamas, yoga clothes, and my yoga mat, I told the cat who'd climbed back in the suitcase, "Out, or I'm zipping you inside."

"You're forgetting one thing." She led me to a pair of pink running shoes in the closet, which looked like they belonged in Ryland's rainbow sneaker collection. "You have pink shoes! And yet you wouldn't buy those gold sneakers yesterday."

"No one should own those sneakers. And thanks, I actually need these running shoes."

We found Ryland looking at my books. "I thought you didn't like fantasy," he said with a tiny smirk.

"Ugh, I hoped you'd forget that. I apologize for lying. Fangirling over fantasy wasn't exactly a welcome conversation topic in my previous circle."

An offended curlicue of smoke twisted from Midnight's nostrils.

Ryland slid a cozy fantasy about a tea shop back onto the shelf. "Sounds like your friends are boring, Kin."

Twilight tittered. "I like him. The dragon too."

So did I. "Let me take the trash down, and we can go."

When I got back upstairs, Ryland had the bookcase in the middle of the room, wrapped in swaths of cerulean magic. "I assume we're taking this and leaving everything else?"

I bit my lip as I walked up to grab the suitcase handle. How did he know that?

"Sorry," he said, misinterpreting my reaction. He squeezed my arm. "Did I assume wrong?"

"No, you're right. You just surprised me."

He lifted his non-dragon-bearing shoulder. "I've been in a lot of people's homes in my career. You get good at interpreting a person's connection to their space. You don't seem particularly attached to any of this stuff. Other than the books."

I cleared my throat, which had felt too thick, too tight. "Yeah, I'm good at that too. I learned to assess a person and their home quickly in foster care. I know it's weird to have so little stuff, but I just...learned not to need it, I guess."

He gave me such an intense look that I needed an immediate subject change. "Hey, it's better than hoarding. I hear Denise hoarded. Did you find anything super weird in her house? Your standard piles of newspapers next to a box of stuffed mice or something?"

He laughed, Midnight chittering along. "If you only kn ew…"

"Oooh, see if he'll tell you anything, Kinley!" Twilight said.

I spun the suitcase in a circle. "C'mon, you can tell me."

He leaned against the bookcase. "Miss Paigewright, are you phishing for information about an active investigation?"

"No, just curious, since I heard about the hoarding."

The detective looked at me for several seconds. "I can't tell you anything, but if I could, I'd tell you that Denise's house was weird as spell but not helpful."

I sighed. "Did you know she's not really divorced? Tabitha told me." I repeated everything the bakery employee had said about Denise's ex, the money, and his new girlfriend.

He pushed off the bookcase. "I didn't know that. Interesting. I'll have to confirm that's accurate, but it changes things."

Good. At least he had one potential suspect other than me now.

"Ready?" he asked, tapping the bookcase.

"Are you sure about moving the whole thing? I can just grab my favorite books."

"Page would never forgive me if I didn't portal all the books home for you."

Home. To Sea Sprite.

I looked out the sliver of exposed window at Portland, my long-time ally, often my only friend.

Ryland turned to look too, his jacket brushing my sweater. After a minute, I brushed the single tear off my cheek.

"Kin, I can bring you to Portland anytime you want. Well, as long as it's not past ten." He leaned in conspiratorially. "You do not want to see me past ten." Midnight flapped his wings. "He agrees. Says I'm grumpier than a declawed griffin after ten."

My laugh filled the empty condo, and I realized I'd laughed more and felt fuller in just a few days in Sea Sprite than years in Portland. And I had a new friend offering to bring me back any time before ten p.m.

"Do me one favor, though," Ryland continued. "Get some groceries. I'll show you the store."

Twilight spun in a circle. "Oh, ragwort and rose, *please* get some groceries. I cannot live off mustard. Do you see this sleek fur? I need fresh fish and chicken. Maybe some ice cream."

I put a hand on my chest. "You want me to have food in the house? That's a terrible sacrifice, Ry, but for you—and Twilight, apparently—I'll do it."

With that, he opened a portal to my grandma's house. *My* house.

Chapter Fourteen

"**W**hat if the police come back while we're inside?" Azura asked, one perfectly plucked brow raised as she watched Denise's house roll into view from the middle row of Miguel's minivan.

"Ryland told me they didn't find anything," I said, pressing my face to the glass of the back row's little window. At least the white paint and white shutters of the craftsman home caught the moonlight, making it easy to see. White on white. Of course Denise's house was boring. Twilight would hate it. It felt odd not to have her here, but tonight was too dicey for familiars. "From his tone, I don't think the MBI plans to return."

"If they do, they'll come through the front." Zori said from the seat next to Miguel. "We can flee through the back, the same way we go in. All those tall trees and the dark will cover us."

Shea reached over from the other middle seat to put a hand on Azura's shoulder. "I can fly away, you and Zori can glamour yourselves, and Kinley can pretend to be on a walk. Detective Fores will just take her for ice cream or something. He already took her *grocery shopping*."

I rolled my eyes. After we'd portaled back earlier, Ryland had dragged me to the grocery store, where he'd judged all my purchases and made me spend more than my usual eight minutes. "He's just being nice. Probably because Midnight and I are besties now."

Miguel snorted from the driver's seat. "Sure, guys usually take women grocery shopping after helping them move *just to be nice*."

Shea fluffed her red curls. "And *he* suggested it."

"Okay," Azura said, her wings beating twice, drawing everyone's attention like the bang of a gavel. "We've now driven several houses past Denise's, and I'm not convinced breaking in is worth the risk."

"C'mon," Shea said, reaching over to squeeze her friend's forearm. "We can't do it without you, Azura."

Literally, as I'd learned earlier that evening.

Once I'd shelved my groceries, I went to the animal shelter to find Shea. Since we hadn't seen anything about Denise's secret business at her shop, I figured it had to be at her house. And now I knew the police hadn't found it. So, *we* needed to try.

No way could I get through Ryland's ward, but I'd hoped Shea could shift and fly through. Nope. She'd informed me only one person could get through wards. Azura.

I bit the corner of my bottom lip. "I get it. I'm asking a lot of you guys. But the MBI doesn't know about Denise's secret business, so they might have missed something about it at her house."

Azura tapped her fingers on her armrest. "True, but if we get caught, we could go to prison."

Zori looked at Azura with grave eyes. "Kinley could go to prison for a lot longer if we don't find the killer. Detective Fores's bosses wanted her interrogated today."

"Half the town already thinks she's guilty too," Miguel added, coming to a stop at the end of the road.

Azura's wings beat one more time. "Oh, hexes. Let's do it."

Miguel dropped us off two streets back and wished us luck. He couldn't stay. If we got caught, it would jeopardize his and Sundar's adoption application, which also explained why they had a minivan.

We weren't far from my house—just a couple streets inland. The properties here lacked fences, their tree-filled yards bleeding into each other. Shea shifted and flew through the branches. Zori cast a spell to hide the rest of us, and we crept through the trees until we reached Denise's yard.

At the ward boundary, Azura pulled in a deep breath. "Just like school, right?"

"If you could do it as an eight-year-old, you can do it now," Shea said.

I brushed debris off my black jeans and black jacket, happy to be in my own warm clothes. "You phased through wards as young as eight?"

Azura smiled. "Our principal took something he shouldn't have."

Shea shifted back and leaned on her cane. "My older brother couldn't function without his favorite hoodie. It was like armor for him. He's autistic, and he got in trouble for wearing the hood up. The principal put it in the warded room full of confiscated items."

"Imagine a bunch of little kids with magic running around doing magical things with magical objects," Zori said, her eyes shining in the moonlight. "The school needed a lot of wards."

"And when they took the hoodie," Azura said, "I decided to test my wings."

Those golden wings began beating until they moved at a pace beyond visible comprehension, stirring up the crisp air. It looked as if her wings had disappeared—a talent quite unique to Azura, apparently. Her speed-of-light flutter was renowned among fairies, but no one knew she could use those wings to rearrange magic, to rapidly move spelled particles to create a gap in wards that wouldn't register as a disturbance.

She backed her tall wings up to the almost invisible dome around the property, and I watched with gleeful amazement as a break formed in the ward. Shea became a raven again and flew through. When the hole grew, Zori grabbed my hand and pulled me inside—and tripped over a twig, bringing us both to the ground.

"Oops!" Zori rolled to her side.

I rubbed my elbow. "No worries, but next time, I'll lead."

Azura managed to step through backward without crushing us under her brown lace-up boots. The gap closed behind her.

Shea flew around the home, checking the neighbor's windows for prying eyes before landing on the deck and giving us a thumbs-up. I led Azura and Zori across the yard, smiling when I noticed fallen leaves that would have annoyed Denise. Everything else had remained pristine in the yard, just as Madam Malfina had said.

The MBI hadn't locked the back door, likely due to the ward's presence, so I strolled right in. And froze, with my companions running into each other behind me.

"Hex me to hoarding spell," I muttered, grateful my migraine had lessened after a nap. I could not handle this otherwise.

Azura, the tallest of us, looked over my head. "*Organized* hoarding."

Boxes, boxes everywhere. Cardboard, plastic, metal. Denise had them all, and she'd stacked them everywhere. Some of the shoe variety, others of the banker style, and even some that looked like they could hold a frickin' exploding bomb.

The moonlight illuminated the kitchen, only a quarter of which could still be said to serve kitchen purposes. The other three quarters—the floor, the table, the counters, the top of the fridge—held well-maintained, recently dusted boxes. Even the bulging cabinets appeared to hold small boxes.

"Wands and willows, this could take all night," Shea said. "Let's do this."

So, we searched by dim witchlights our witchy partner in crime spelled to follow each of us.

Zori and I started in what may have once been a living room but was now a recliner surrounded by boxes of outlandish items.

After an hour, we'd found singing vintage potion labels that only carried a semblance of their original spells and now warbled their potion names in slow, funereal tones; mini snow globes, which upon dropping, I discovered played scenes from the movie *Saturday Night Fever*; a case of magical kaleidoscopes that almost made me hurl; *so many* 1980s baseball cards that carried no magic whatsoever; two wearable crystal balls, in case you needed to tell *two* fortunes on the go; a box of carefully wrapped, taxidermied rodents; a nearby case of tiny clothes I suspected was for said creepy-as-curses rodents; and *so much more*.

"This sucks," Shea called, coming to lean on the bottom newel post, just visible through the living room's entryway. "I can't believe MBI officers do this all the time. If I see one more crate of whistling watches or squirrel pelts, I'm burning this house down."

With that, she went upstairs. "Hey, guess what? More boxes. More boxes. Barely even a bed. More boxes. *Whoa.*"

I pushed to my feet. "What?"

"There's a room *not* full of a serial killer's trash."

Azura came running from the kitchen, and we all rushed up the steps, our witchlights bobbing above us. We found Shea in the middle of a small room, her curls casting twisting shadows under her light. She stood near a large antique desk—the only piece of furniture in the room besides the accompanying chair. The walls held no art on the wood paneling. No rug sat on the wood floor.

"Why is this room empty?" Azura asked. "Why not the bedroom, of all the rooms?"

I approached the bare desk, running a finger over the freshly polished surface. "It's clean like at her shop. I think Denise had two modes: work and home. She worked in this room."

Moving behind the desk, Shea said, "And why have a second office, if not for nefarious activities?" Shea started opening drawers on the left side, so I took the right. Zori stayed on the opposite side, whispering spells over the desk while flourishing her wand.

Four wide, deep drawers sat stacked in my half. I started with the bottom, pulling out bundles of what felt like ordinary, thick cardstock. After checking each sheet, I pulled out the drawer and checked for a false bottom. Nothing.

The next three drawers held pens, scissors, knives, ribbons. And no false bottoms.

Letting my butt fall into the chair, I said, "I've got nothing."

"Same," Shea said.

Zori muttered one more spell, then huffed a frustrated sigh. "I can't find any magic here. What do you think, Azura?" No reply. "Wait, where is she?"

We located her crouched beside an interior wall, her wings tucked, her hand caressing the wood paneling. Azura's pointed ears twitched in time with her silently moving lips.

"Azura?" Zori whispered as she approached her on tiptoes and dropped into a squat, but of course, she lost her balance and fell right into Azura.

Who fell *through the wall.*

Zori jumped up. "Gah! Did I do that somehow?"

Azura's head popped out of the wall, her gold-dusted braids swinging. "Nope. That was me. It's a false wall. Come through."

The four of us crammed into the three-foot-wide space, our lights following us inside. Shelves climbed from floor to ceiling on both ends.

"Denise somehow got hold of old fairy magic, grown into the wood itself," Azura explained. "The wood paneling is walnut, which has natural protection properties, but snapdragon flowers grew alongside it to imbue it with concealment magic, which was further enhanced by the fairies who nurtured it long ago. The MBI's standard fairy-magic detectors wouldn't have caught something this innate. Most fairies wouldn't have either, and the local MBI office hasn't even had a fairy officer since Poppy retired."

Shea clapped Azura on the arm. "Your talents are really coming in handy tonight."

"Seriously," I agreed. "Look at all this. You found the jackpot." I walked to the shelves on one end. "Are these potion ingredients?"

Zori and Azura reached around me to pluck some of the bottles.

"Yes, and some of them are *vile*," Zori said.

She moved to pick up another bottle, but Azura grabbed her hand. "Maybe don't pick up any of the super poisonous ingredients, okay? We don't need any accidents."

"Why would Denise have poisons?" I squeaked out, my breaths coming faster.

Azura bent to look at the middle shelf where Denise had set a tray with a two-inch lip and a clear plastic lid. I lowered myself as well. Violet liquid covered the bottom inch, a piece of paper floating inside. At the top of the sheet, I caught the words, "From the desk of Mr. Deed."

"Do. Not. Touch. That." Azura said, her voice echoing in the small space. "Mr. Deed may have become Mr. Dead if his stationary sat in that poison any longer. I doubt she meant to let it cook this long."

On that note, I backed away from them and joined Shea's search at the other set of shelves. The top shelf held more paper, but unlike the paper in the desk drawers, it carried a slight buzz to it. "I think this paper has a spell on it."

"You would know, muffin," Shea said. "Open your senses. Free your bibliomancy. How does the spell feel?"

I set the pages down. "Nope. I don't need to blow up this room full of poison ingredients."

She put a hand on her hip. "Kinley, just feel it, girl. Just let the magic come to you."

Grumbling, I pulled one sheet off the pile and let it sit on my palm. After a few seconds, I felt my magic tingle. "I think this paper somehow ceases to exist after it's read by the intended recipient."

"Yes!" She bumped me with her shoulder, which in the small space, jostled me against the wall.

I smiled. "No one died! Let's keep going."

The next shelf held envelopes clearly meant to pair with the paper. An entire shelf beneath held small glass bottles about the size of a film canister. About half held clear, viscous liquid. I held one in my palm and somehow knew it to be invisible ink.

"Ink, paper...it's all part of bibliomancy," Shea said when I told her.

She handed me a bottle of blue liquid, which I recognized as a compulsion ink. "Ugh, she was getting paid to compel people to do things. Gross."

I lifted one of the third and final types, of which Denise had ten bottles. The black ink looked oily in a way that didn't seem conducive to writing. I held it for a full minute, but I had no idea what it did. Shea leaned in. "My shifter nose detects the ocean. Weird."

Azura and Zori couldn't identify it either, though they had found more terrible potion ingredients and a few more in-progress cursed paper products.

"Well, Tyler was right," I said. "This is a lot worse than cheating on exams. Do you think Denise killed anyone?"

Zori shook her head. "The curses aren't strong enough for that, except for the eruere curse on Mr. Deed's stationery, but like Azura said, I'm guessing Denise only meant that to brew overnight. It would have made him super ill, but not killed him."

I decided not to ask what the curse did.

"That's good, I guess. Any other targets named, or just Mr. Deed?"

Azura shook her head. "No records at all."

We hadn't seen any on our shelves either. Denise had several ledgers at her shop, but would she really keep her criminal records there? Even if she did mix the records, I hadn't seen anything in them to tell me who had placed orders for corrupt paper products.

"There's a torn envelope on the floor over here," Shea said, pointing under the bottom shelf. "I'm afraid to touch it. I don't want to end up like Almost Mr. Dead."

Zori raised her wand, and the envelope followed. She flicked it and the piece of paper inside shot out and unfolded.

Neat, loopy letters in a matte scarlet ink declared:

Denise,

If I could have cursed this letter like you cursed my sister, I would have. But I'll have my revenge. One day, when you're walking in those ugly shoes, thinking about which cookie you might have that night, I'll come out of nowhere. You'll never see me, never hear me coming.

-T

A bead of sweat caressed my spine, the tiny room suddenly stifling. Did we just read the killer's words?

"Mother of the moon," Shea said. She held her phone up to take a few photos of the letter. "This could be from the murderer...and we can't tell the MBI. Not without risking prison ourselves."

"Which means we have to solve this," I concluded.

"C'mon," Azura said. "We got what we needed."

Zori flicked her wand again, the letter folded itself back into the envelope and dropped to the floor. But it still tugged at me, like an invisible lasso of ink pulled me to it. So when everyone turned to leave the room, I slipped the letter into my pocket, somehow knowing it wouldn't hurt me.

Chapter Fifteen

"Oh, this feels so good!" Sylvie rocked side to side on her back, feet raised to the cloudy sky, hands clasped around her toes. "You called this position 'happy baby?'"

I reveled in the stretch in my thighs as I pulled my legs a bit higher. "Yep, it's one of my favorite yoga poses. Just grabbin' onto your feet like a baby." The waves crashed behind us, and I closed my eyes, soaking in the sound.

My migraine had resolved by the morning, and with the typical Oregon clouds blocking the sun above, I'd decided some outdoor yoga wouldn't trigger a new one—though I'd armed myself with dark glasses just in case. I'd been about to head to the backyard to set up just beyond the fire pit when the doorbell rang. Sylvie had flown over with a bag of muffins, but when she'd seen my yoga mat, she'd soared home to change so she could join me.

"I might not have thumbs to do this right, but this position still does wonders for my back."

Turning to Twilight, I said, "We should get you a yoga mat."

Her four skyward feet twitched. "Kinley, oh my god, can it be yellow plaid like—"

"Like Cher's skirt in *Clueless*?" I released my legs and turned to Sylvie. "Any idea where I can get a yellow plaid yoga mat?"

She laughed, the sound carrying on the ocean breeze. "Magic can make that happen."

Twilight flipped over and did a happy jig.

I calmed her and guided us all into corpse pose, where we simply laid on our backs. Dusk had already put herself in corpse pose ten minutes early, having tired of yoga well before the rest of us. The raccoon looked adorable snoring on her back next to Sylvie.

For our last pose, we curled on our sides. Then, with a full heart and limber muscles, I rose and turned to the ocean. "What...*wow*."

"Cool!" Twilight said. "They're so beautiful!"

Twelve winged beings hovered ten feet from us. The mist that seemed to perpetually engulf the coast had followed them, twining around their six-inch bodies. If not for their dusty-purple glow, which grew darker around their wings until it reached an almost black, they would have faded into the gray mist.

Sylvie put a hand on her chest. "The Sea Sprites have honored us with their presence."

As the sprites moved closer, their wings beating slower than I'd have expected, the air grew icy. The closest one smiled and bowed.

I tugged the cuffs of my slate-gray crewneck sweatshirt over my hands and bowed in return, my side braid tickling my chin. "It's nice to meet you."

Twilight lowered herself into a kitty bow. "Thank you for coming."

The sprites waved to her before they moved in a choreographed, fanciful retreat, the mist withdrawing as they danced away.

"They're amazing," I said. "I hadn't seen them yet."

Sylvie nodded. "They stick to the forested shores of the island where they can really hide in the mist. Sea Sprites are endangered, and they have a lot of poachers. We protect them here. This island belongs to them more than any of us."

Twilight choked out, "Poachers? People kill them?" which I repeated for Sylvie.

"They steal them, imprison them," Sylvie responded. "You may have noticed they didn't speak. By choice, they only speak to impart visions. They're powerful seers, but they choose when and for whom they see. Poachers take them and force them to work or they use the sprite's secretions—a dew that forms in their wings and has foresight properties."

Anger burned up any lingering chill in my body. "Okay, I hate that. If I see a poacher, I'm going to throw a thousand books at them or something."

"I'll tear their eyes out with my claws!" Twilight said.

"It's awful," Sylvie said. "But the MBI does a good job of protecting the sprites. Powerful wards prevent anyone from taking a sprite through the isle's portal or through the boundary."

"Boundary?" I asked.

"The magical dome that keeps Sea Sprite Isle hidden from humans."

That made sense.

Sylvie bent to wake Dusk. "Well, shall we go inside?"

"One second." I ran upstairs and came back with my cell phone. Sylvie took hers out, probably thinking we'd finally exchange numbers, but I walked right past her to the edge of the lawn where the grass dropped off to the ocean several feet below.

And threw my phone in.

I didn't know who'd contacted me after my wedding disaster, and now I'd never know. Maybe my former colleagues. Maybe even one of Aaron's sisters. But I didn't need to know.

Twilight wove in and out of my feet, cackling like the Wicked Witch of the West. "Yes! Can we throw more stuff in?"

Sylvie came to stand beside me and pulled me into a side hug. "Does it feel good to release your old life?"

"Spell yes. I do need a phone, though. With a new number. Can you point me in the right direction?"

An hour later, Sylvie and I stood on the sidewalk in front of our shops. My new phone mostly worked like a human-world phone, but Sylvie had needed to explain the extra apps, like the Magical Positioning System, which helped plan routes to or from magical locations.

I scrunched up my nose. "So, to go to Bellingham, I'd have to take a portal, then get on a broomstick or on a magical bus unless I want to switch to human transportation at—"

"Oooh, look, it's Ryland and Midnight!"

I looked up from the phone to see Twilight pointing a paw at her two new favorite beings standing in front of Mystic Mugs. A tendril of warmth curled around my heart when Ryland planted a kiss on Midnight's cheek.

A gangly Latino man of about fifty years old approached Ryland with his hand held out. "Ryland, how's your mother?" the man asked, the booming words carrying down the sidewalk.

Sylvie grabbed my arm. "That's Denise's ex-husband, Chris. He's so nice. I'll never understand why he stayed with her for so long."

"They weren't actually divorced!" I quickly explained what Tabitha told me as the men exchanged a few more words before heading inside the coffee shop. "Ryland must want to ask him about it."

"Stay here!" With Dusk around her neck, Sylvie zipped inside Pegasus Potions, which two of her employees had just opened for the day. She came back out with two small vials. "Let's go."

She led me into Mystic Mugs, where a long line stretched almost to the door. Ryland and Chris had by-passed it and headed straight for a corner table. Sylvie walked with confident steps to a chair three tables down and sat. Dusk crawled onto the table and fell asleep.

I took the chair across from her. "Are we spying? Because I don't think I can hear from here." Chris's voice had lowered, and only a few words reached me.

Sylvie knocked back one of the vials she held before handing me the other. "Take a few deep breaths once it hits."

That did not make me want to swallow the clear liquid, but I did anyway. Sylvie hadn't steered me wrong so far.

A coffee shop is not the best location for one's first hearing enhancement potion. Especially when one has sound sensitivity already—thanks, migraines.

It only took a single instant for me to become overwhelmed by the grind and scream of the espresso machine, by the screech of chairs, by the slamming of everything. Doors, hands, phones on tables.

Twilight climbed up my sweatshirt and pressed into my neck.

"Breathe," Sylvie reminded me, the word as loud as the other jumble of voices around us—a few of which gossiped about *me*, the murderer.

I forced myself to suck in a breath, then another. It helped me separate the sounds a little better, but not enough to keep me from teetering on the edge of panic.

Then I heard the smallest meep to my left, like Midnight knew I could only handle the barest of sound from him, followed by, "Breathe, Kinley" in a low whisper from Ryland.

I moved just my eyes to see Ryland alone at his table. "Breathe, Kinley," he said again.

When I did, my lungs finally absorbed it, and I relaxed. The sounds eased, and I could isolate those I wanted.

"Unbelievable, Sylvie." Now, Ryland sounded like one seriously pissed off detective.

Chris came back from the bathrooms a minute later. "Sorry about that. Okay, what do you need to ask me?"

Ryland wasted no time. "I thought you and Denise had completed your divorce, but you never filed the paperwork. Why, Chris?"

Denise's ex sighed and rolled up the cuffs of his henley. "You knew Denise. No task could be simple, even taking out the trash. So a divorce? She drew it out, made it painful." He pointed to his slightly receding hairline. "Do you see this? I had more hair before we started divorce proceedings. After a while, I couldn't take it anymore. I realized that legal freedom from her came at a steep price, and I didn't need it. We could stay separated. I let her take the house, the money, everything."

Ryland nodded. "Okay. Did you resent her for making things so challenging?"

"Of course. I won't coat it in pixie dust, detective. I still carry resentment." He shrugged. "Who wouldn't? Money is tight on my own. Starting over is expensive. But I got to be with my girlfriend and away from Denise. I found that well worth the cost."

Tapping his fingers on the table, which sounded like tapping directly on my brain, Ryland assessed him. "Did Denise handle your new relationship okay?"

"Not at first, but she felt like she won when I dropped my divorce petition. Denise's presence as my wife prevented me from marrying my girlfriend, so she left us alone, imagining that we were constantly pining for a marriage certificate."

"And are you?"

Chris waved him off. "Not at all. Neither of us wants to get married ever again. My girlfriend had a failed marriage too. Now, detective, why don't you ask for my alibi?"

Ryland chuckled. "Okay, go ahead. Tell me."

Chris pulled out his phone and showed Ryland proof of a trip with his girlfriend. They'd taken a long weekend to another magical town in Europe that required four portals to travel to from Sea Sprite. "You'll find all the portal records, of course, but I'll send you these hotel docs too. Check my CharmChat for photos."

Ryland nodded. "Thanks, Chris. You know I had to ask."

"I get it. Anything else?"

"Yes. Can you think of anyone who would want to hurt Denise, or anyone who had an issue with her?"

Chris let out a "HA!" that bounced off the rafters and my skull. "Ryland—" apparently he was back to *Ryland* instead of *detective* now that they'd moved on from Chris as a potential suspect—"half this town had an issue with her."

"True, but did anyone stand out?"

"Her neighbors probably hated her the most, since she spent half her time at home glaring at them. Especially the closer ones. Oh! Bethina Solanum really hated Denise too. I caught them arguing in the backyard once, which was really weird. No one came to our house after Denise's hoarding escalated. Denise wouldn't tell me why they fought. Something about business. Maybe Denise made something for Bethina's mayoral campaign and she wasn't happy? I never knew much about the business."

Good for him. Chris seemed like a nice guy, and I hoped he hadn't known anything about Denise's illegal activities.

Chris snapped his fingers before grabbing his wrist. "Do you know about Denise's injury?"

Ryland did indeed know about Denise's slow-to-heal wrist. "Do you know how Denise injured it, Chris?" He leaned in. "It had to be *something* magical." Ryland's tone implied he thought *someone* magical might be responsible.

"I don't know," Chris said. "When I ran into Denise, she tried to hide it from me. I pressured her, and all she'd tell me is that she'd made a mistake."

Did that mean she'd broken her own wrist? Or had she made a mistake with one of her secret orders and gotten herself a snapped bone in return?

"Interesting," Ryland said. "I appreciate your time, Chris. If you think of anything else, please let me know."

The men shook hands and parted ways. A moment later, Ryland used his wand to soundlessly move a third chair to our little table. He slid into it, his jeans brushing against my black leggings.

Ryland crossed his arms and looked at Sylvie. She stared back.

"My money's on the detective to hold out longer," Twilight said, and thank frick, the potion hadn't amplified her voice. Unlike with Page, it didn't *feel* like she spoke inside my head, but I guess she did.

"You could have blocked us with a ward!" Sylvie finally whispered, the words rushing out.

"I win!" Twilight said, proud she'd correctly called which side would break first.

Ryland sighed and took Midnight from his pocket. He set the dragon down and stroked his tail. "I know. You also could have given Kinley more warning about the potion."

"Yeah," I said, my words quiet as I rubbed my jaw. "I think I need a headache potion now."

"That I can do," Sylvie said as she stood. "I'll get a reversal potion for our hearing too."

Twilight curled up around Midnight. Dusk woke long enough to join the cuddle puddle.

"Ask him about Bethina Solanum," Twilight said. "Whoever she is, we need a handwriting sample to compare to the note you all found last night."

"Genius!" I patted her head.

"What?" Ryland asked.

"Oh, just Twilight's idea to, umm, start an ocean side yoga club." I couldn't exactly tell him about the note.

He stretched his arms overhead. "That sounds amazing. I haven't done yoga in a while."

"Sylvie and I did it this morning, and the waves were so therapeutic. I even threw my phone into them."

I showed him my shiny new phone in its purple case. He took it and added his number. "Let me know about yoga."

Twilight and Midnight both made little tittering sounds. I cleared my throat. "So, who's Bethina?"

"She's the town dentist and a former mayoral candidate. Dr. Solanum pulled out of the race a couple months before the election to focus on expanding her dental practice. People come through the portal from all over to see her. She's big on CharmChat."

"So if I find a hot doc in Canada I want to see, I can just portal on up there?"

He reined in his laugh to keep the sound down. "You sure can. It just might take several portals unless you ask me really nicely to take you."

I twirled my braid. "Can you really open a portal to anywhere?"

A suspicious line formed between his brows. "Yes. Why?"

With a smirk, I pointed to the door. "Great, because Sylvie's outside with the potions, and I'd love a portal to the dentist."

Chapter Sixteen

"**D**id the yoga knock loose your logic, Kin?" Ryland leaned against the front of The Perfect Page, shaking his head as I drank my headache potion. "I can't take a suspect to talk to another suspect."

Midnight let out a chastising coil of smoke.

"You know I'm not a real suspect," I argued as the pain in my head cleared. I'd already downed the reversal potion to return my hearing to normal.

Sylvie took the empty vial from me. Apparently, she cleaned and reused them. Dusk leaned down from her neck to sniff it. "I'm with Ryland on this one. Do you want his MBI bosses to skewer him?"

"Sorry," Twilight said, "but I agree with them too. He already let us listen to his interview. Don't get our new friend into trouble!"

I straightened my sweatshirt. "No. You're right. Sorry, Ry."

He pushed off the bricks. "Thanks. Trust me to do my job, okay?"

With that, he opened a portal and stepped through.

Trust wasn't the issue. Ryland didn't have all the facts. He hadn't found Denise's hidden room, didn't know about her illicit activities. I couldn't tell him without getting us all in trouble.

"I think my tooth hurts," I told Sylvie. "Where can I find the dentist?"

With a sly smile, she said, "Oh no, how terrible. If you walk down Toil, you'll pass the town hall and the grocery store before you reach a medical complex. You'll find Dr. Solanum there."

Page's low timber warmed me. *I take it we need to post-pone our lesson?*

I looked up at the bookstore's awning. *Yes, sorry! I'll be back later. I promise.*

Before the mission to Denise's house the night before, Page and I had resumed lessons about the shop. We'd planned to keep going today.

Good. We still have things to cover before opening tomorrow for your first day.

My teeth found the inside of my cheek and clamped down. Generations of Paigewrights had run this store. I didn't want to disappoint them. Shaking off my nerves, I said, *I can't wait.*

Page laughed, the sound like rippling paper. *Yes, I can sense your excitement.*

Note to self: You can't lie to the sentient shop knit into your soul.

I turned to leave, but Page said, *You have a far walk, unless you use your grandmother's bicycle.*

Turning to Sylvie, I said, "Margaret had a bicycle?"

She'd been absentmindedly stroking Dusk's tail as Page and I talked, but now she smiled. "Yes. She loved it. You can find it in the shed out back. Flying was a passion of hers, but she enjoyed the exercise of riding a bicycle."

"Brooms and I will not be friends, but a bicycle? Heck yeah. Twilight, let's go."

Twenty minutes later, we rode up the hill from our house toward Toil Avenue. The ivory beach cruiser with brown accents rode like a dream. Even the helmet I'd found molded perfectly to me—because even witches needed to protect their noggins. Twilight sat in a basket on the front that had shrunk to fit her frame, keeping her nice and cozy. I hoped it would expand to fit bigger items as well. Another spell must have made riding uphill easier too, because I barely had to push the pedals.

Dr. Solanum's office had a bike rack out front, so I engaged the magical lock I'd discovered with the bicycle and put the helmet in the basket. I half expected the inside of the unassuming white building to have twirling teeth everywhere, like a magical dental musical, but the inside looked like every dentist ever.

Twilight sat at my feet as I leaned on the tall front counter and clutched the left side of my face. "Hello. I'm new to town, and I have a toothache. Any chance the dentist could squeeze me in?" I pulled my face into a wince for good measure.

The employee flashed their pearly whites, and I almost fainted from the fluorescents reflecting off them. Hexes, did the employee benefits include a whitening treatment every *day*?

"You're in luck. Someone canceled twenty minutes ago for their appointment that starts on the hour." They plopped a clipboard down. "Fill these out, please."

Exactly on the hour, they took me back to a room filled with instruments that looked similar to human-world dentistry implements.

I sat in the massive chair, and Twilight curled up on my lap. After just a few minutes, an assistant came in, tilted me back, and the machines started moving of their own accord. Diving into my mouth to take X-rays. Measuring the spaces in between my teeth. Poking at my molars. I clung to Twilight, who they'd allowed to stay with me, but I relaxed after a few minutes. Especially when I realized there'd be no glaring lights in my face. I guess the magic didn't need them.

Only moments after the assistant left, a pale white fairy with shimmering silver wings and matching silver hair entered. She looked about forty and wore a huge smile, and though she revealed bright-white teeth, they didn't threaten to destroy my retinas like her receptionist's had. "Good morning! You got so lucky to get this appointment. I hope you haven't been in pain for too long." She went straight to a laptop in the corner and opened a file. "I'm Dr. Solanum, it's nice to meet you..." Her eyes searched the screen. "Oh." She turned and ran her eyes over my face and black braid. "Sorry, umm, it's nice to meet you, Kinley."

"She recognizes you!" Twilight said, her tail swishing across my sweatshirt. "Use it. Make a joke."

I held my hand out. "You too. Don't worry. Only one person I've met in Sea Sprite has ended up dead on my porch. Most likely, you'll be fine."

"Oof," Twilight said. "That's the joke you went with?"

With a wince, I let my hand drop. "Sorry. Everyone thinks I killed Denise, which has made things awkward for me. I didn't mean to make such an insensitive joke."

Dr. Solanum stepped closer and held her hand out. "It's fine. If someone else had died, maybe I'd take offense, but Denise doesn't deserve my pity or outrage."

We shook. "Thanks, doctor. It's been hard having people think I killed someone I just met. I'd only been in town for a few hours when Denise and I fought, and I hadn't even been here for twenty-four hours when she died."

She leaned against the counter across from the chair. "Denise had a way of upsetting people. I'm sure she meant to antagonize you the moment she realized who you were." Dr. Solanum pursed her lips. "I barely knew her, but I think she made it her goal in life to one-up as many people as possible."

"It sounds like you have experience."

Turning to a pile of instruments, she gave me a brief nod. "Yes, so I feel for you."

"What happened?"

Dr. Solanum's wings sagged. "Denise came to me for dental work. She complained about every aspect of the process. We did our best to accommodate her requests. In the end, she still found herself unhappy. She bad-mouthed our practice around town and online. I asked her to stop, but she refused. Eventually, I accepted it. We have enough goodwill with customers that I had to hope one unhappy customer, no matter how vocal, wouldn't affect us too much."

That sounded exactly like what Denise would do. It should be easy to corroborate, if I could find where Denise posted online.

"Anyway," the doctor's smile returned. "Tell me where it hurts."

I pointed out a tooth on the bottom left of my mouth. She snapped her fingers and her instruments pried back my cheeks. A little mirror zoomed into my mouth. I shut my eyes as she engaged a flashlight to look at the tooth that didn't hurt at all.

After a few moments, she walked back to the laptop and pulled up my X-rays and the other readings the earlier instruments had taken. "Everything looks good. I don't see anything at all to suggest an issue with that particular tooth. How long have you been in pain?"

"A few days. Since I got to Sea Sprite. Oh, what's that, Twilight?" I looked down at my silent familiar before lifting my eyes back to Dr. Solanum. "My familiar wonders if it could be from my migraines. I get jaw pain but usually not pain concentrated to one tooth."

"Good thought." She smiled at Twilight. "Your migraines could absolutely cause pain like this. Our instruments are quite thorough, so I think we can safely rule out a dental issue with that tooth. It's possible the migraine pain has simply spread a bit."

I cringed. "That's not good. I appreciate your help, though. At least now I know."

"Of course, Kinley."

I moved to stand.

"Wait, we aren't done. While that tooth is fine, your gums need a little work."

What? I had a rigorous oral hygiene routine. I brushed for two minutes with an electric toothbrush. I flossed. I used fancy mouthwash.

She chuckled. "You look surprised. Don't worry; it happens to the best of us." A cabinet above her contained several rows of neon-pink bottles. "Make sure you floss, or better yet, use a water-based dental flosser." She handed me a bottle. "This mouthwash will help too. Just one bottle should do it. Use it twice a day, thirty seconds at a time."

I accepted the bottle. "I feel like I got a failing grade on a paper."

"Ha, you sound like me. Anyway, we book up quickly, so set up an appointment for a routine cleaning on your way out. We can check your gums then."

Twilight dug her claws into my leggings, and I hissed. "Sorry," she said. "But we need to check her handwriting."

Right, we needed to compare it to the threatening letter at Denise's. "Before I go, could you write down the instructions?"

Dr. Solanum tilted her head.

"For the mouthwash," I clarified. "You said twenty seconds, once a day? Or was it thirty seconds? I have a terrible memory."

"Ah, I see." She grabbed a sticky note and scrawled it down for me.

I thanked her, and looked at the note, relieved that the tidy, tight letters didn't match those from the threatening letter.

"We don't know the killer sent that letter," Twilight reminded me as I set her in the bike's basket a few minutes later. "Someone other than the killer could have sent it, which means Dr. Solanum could still have killed Denise."

Sighing, I swung my leg over the bike and clipped my helmet on. "I guess we better get on the internet—or is it the witchernet?—and figure out when Denise tried to tank Dr. Solanum's practice."

Chapter Seventeen

"Wow, Denise started a hashtag to tank Dr. Solanum?" I scrolled on my newly installed CharmChat app, with Shea looking over my shoulder. "Of course, she's the only one who posted to it. It looks like she stopped posting six months ago."

I clicked on one of Denise's posts. A few people chimed in with disparaging comments about Sea Sprite's dentist, but most told Denise to back off Dr. Solanum.

Shea chuckled. "Did you see this one from emmypie34 calling Denise a parasitical drain on the magical world?"

"Ouch. Twistiewistie95 has that beat with 'Denise, go shave your head, you fleabag.' That's really harsh. The witchernet sucks as much as the internet."

Shea clapped me on the back. "Yep. We don't call it the witchernet, though. Now, let's go meet Zori and Azura."

After collecting a sleeping Twilight from under one of The Perfect Page's armchairs, Shea and I stepped into a light evening breeze. I held the cat in one arm so I could lock the door. We crossed the street to The Witch Stitch, dodging one of the town's self-pedaling pedicabs.

"Careful, dears!" called Madam Malfina from inside the passenger compartment. She gave us a wave as the three-wheeled bicycle carried her away. Part of me wanted to try one of the driverless contraptions, but most of me still didn't trust magic enough. I'd stick with my bicycle to get home after this next adventure.

When I'd told the gals the night before that I'd opted to leave my stuffy clothes behind in Portland, they'd insisted on taking me shopping at the clothing store catty-corner to the bookshop. Shea had arrived just as Page finished showing me how to order new books from suppliers. While he could organize the shop and access the records, he left spending and tracking money to me.

"Kinley! Shea!" I looked up to see an airborne Zori zooming toward us from past the clothing store, where Trouble Avenue shifted to more residential buildings. She did a loop on her broom before shifting into a complicated spiral that reminded me of a triple Axel in ice skating. With masterful command of her craft, Zori came out of the maneuver and dove to the ground, pulling up just in time to land next to us. She pushed back a pair of purple goggles to reveal shining eyes and glowing pink cheeks.

"Whoa," I breathed. "You really are a pro."

Zori held out her arms, broom still gripped in one hand, and bowed. "Told you."

Sunset stuck his head out of a backpack strapped to her shoulders, and I smiled. It must carry a spell to keep the red panda safely inside.

"I love your broom." My hand moved of its own accord, drawn in by the thick, twisted transparent handle with a large curlicue at the end that brought the wind to mind. I pulled my fingers back, unsure if I should touch another's broom. "It doesn't have any bristles."

"Kinley." Her lips twitched. "Broom innovation moved past bristles a long time ago. We don't need to sweep with them, after all. Some witches still prefer the classic look, but a lot of us opt for something fancier." She pushed a button on the broom and it collapsed to a size small enough to fit in her bag.

I nodded. "Makes sense."

A light dusting of gold powder on my arms had me gazing skyward again, this time finding Azura slowly descending, her gorgeous wings flapping behind her. Unlike Zori, she wore no protective covering on her face. Azura adjusted her olive-green bomber jacket when she landed. "It's chilly up there." She knocked her shoulder into mine. "You ready for this?"

"Almost."

A snore drew our attention to the furball in my arms. I leaned down to whisper in my familiar's twitching ear. "Twilight? Wake up! It's makeover time."

Her eyes shot open faster than Zori could fly. "What? Oh. My. Cauldrons." She climbed the front of my sweatshirt and stuck her face in mine. "Are you serious? You better not be messing with me."

We all laughed. "Yes. We made plans last night after we left Denise's house. I didn't tell you—so it would be a surprise. Let's go!"

The Witch Stitch's front windows had led me to expect a normal clothing store. Well, other than the moving mannequins. But when I stepped inside, I realized this was no department store.

Under a canopy of blinking stars on a black ceiling floated individual pieces of clothing at just under my eye level. No designations between genders marked the store, but items with similar themes hovered together. Floral tops. Black pants. Thick sweaters. Only one of each item.

"Welcome, welcome!" a bright voice called from the depths of the expansive space as wide and deep as the bookshop. A moment later, a woman in her fifties emerged, the clothes gracefully moving out of her way. "Oh, it's you three." She high-fived my companions and high-pawed Sunset before turning to me. The tall, Black witch smiled and held out a hand. "I'm Lacey Weaver, the owner."

"Kinley Paigewright," I said, shaking her hand. "This is Twilight," I said, gesturing to the cat, who seemed to have forgotten how to form words as she stared open-mouthed at the designs above her. Sunset crawled out of Zori's bag to join Twilight in gaping.

Lacey's topaz eyes bulged just a bit. "Margaret's grand-daughter."

"I'm not a murderer!" I blurted.

She snorted and put her hands on her wide hips, drawing my attention to the A-line sea-green dress she wore. For a second I thought the hem swayed, but then I realized small waves crashed along the bottom of the dress. "I didn't think you were. Someone clearly tried to frame you." Lacey examined me, and I suddenly felt self-conscious in my yoga clothes. "Should we get some new clothes on that *frame*?" She let out a laugh that filled the room. "I'm too funny. C'mon, point out some things you like."

Hints of purple shone in her black curls as she turned to lead us through the shop. I wrung my hands, a bit uncertain of what new style I wanted. In Twilight's words, "boring as barf" had been my style for quite some time.

"Kinley! Look!" Twilight jumped on all four paws, her nose directed at a hot-pink strapless dress.

Azura noticed the hearts in my familiar's eyes. "Twi-light, you have a good eye, but that color would wash out Kinley's skin tone. Maybe we can find a different shade of pink for your witch."

My cat hung her head but moved on, and Azura winked at me.

Lacey didn't take me to any neon colors, thank frick. We looked at a range of fabrics and patterns. I vetoed anything too revealing or too stiff. After ten minutes or so, she had a squad of sweaters and blouses floating behind her. "I'll start you a dressing room and search for additional pieces.

You ladies should look around to see what else you can find too."

Twilight, of course, kept leading me to loud patterns, but my new pals proved to have better taste. Azura presented me with a high-necked black top with white polka dots that even my flashy familiar liked. Sunset helped Zori choose a mauve V-neck blouse with buttons down the back that, while pink, didn't meet Twilight's qualifications for pink. I loved the buttons, though. Shea stunned me with a long-sleeve blouse in the same green as my eyes that had a sparse pattern of tiny gold unicorns that *moved*. I'd steered clear of most of the enchanted pieces, but something about this one, maybe the color, called to me.

Lacey called us to a wide, bright-white dressing room. She stooped to pat my familiar on the head. "Ready for a fashion show, Twilight?"

The cat spun in circles. "Yesyesyesyesyes!"

"First up," Lacey announced, flicking her wand, "a wickedly soft sweater with wide-legged jeans." The clothes floated down, and I smiled at the jewel-toned pink sweater Lacey had found.

"Twilight, I think we can both get behind that shade." The top paused in front of me and I plucked it from the air. "Umm, did you guess my size, Lacey?" I didn't see a tag at the collar, but whatever the size, it looked off.

The owner laughed. "My magic needs no sizes. The clothes conform to you. I promise, when you slip that on, it will shape itself to the right size. The cut might not be right for you, but that's different."

I should have known. Sure enough, when I entered the dressing room and changed, the clothes fit. Lacey had me come back outside and do a little runway walk.

"Those pants are too wide for your booty," Shea said, leaning on her cane as she tugged on the fabric.

"But the sweater looks divine," Zori said, pinching the soft fabric between her fingers.

Lacey waved her wand, and the same piece in a soft blue soared over to us. "An air witch needs this shade of blue, Zori."

I insisted we both get the sweater, something Aaron's circle in Portland would have clucked about. If Zori and I wore it on the same day, we could just laugh about it.

An hour later, I had a pile of high-waisted jeans, chunky sweaters, flowy blouses, and the three tops my friends recommended. I kept my last outfit—a boxy camel-brown cardigan with oversize buttons and light jeans—on for the trip home.

At the checkout counter, Shea swung an arm around my neck. "So, you've got a new house, new business, new bicycle, new familiar, new phone, new clothes. How do you feel?"

"Weird. Part of me feels like I'm on some reality TV show, just waiting for a producer to pull the magic carpet out from under me. The rest of me feels at home and more at ease than I have in…maybe ever. I just wish I had family left in Sea Sprite."

I'd dreamed about my parents the night before, or what my subconscious thought they might look like. Twilight had found me crying. She'd promised never to leave me, curled up on top of my head, and snored up a storm.

Lacey stopped wrapping my purchases to wipe a tear off her cheek. "Sorry. Your mother and I grew up together. Next-door neighbors. Good friends." She set her shaking hands on the white counter. "I tried so hard to find her."

Shea pulled me closer, while Zori and Azura instantly came to my back. Twilight climbed onto my shoulder. I took steadying breaths for a few seconds before reaching out to clasp one of Lacey's hands. "Her disappearance must have been so hard for you."

"Honey, this has been harder for you than anyone. But, yes. I portaled to every magical town to search. Sought every seer I could find." She shook her head, her curls bouncing. "I should have known that no one could see more than Madam Malfina."

"Oh! Sylvie told me a seer had only a small vision that I'd been separated from my parents. That was her?"

Lacey nodded. "You can ask Martha about it. I'm sure she'd tell you everything she saw. She keeps irregular business hours now, though."

Zori sighed. "Poor Martha. She's been so sad since the death of her son."

I sucked in a breath. "Oh no. How did he die?"

"An accident," Lacey said. "He was out walking on a remote part of the beach, and a section of the cliffs came down on him. By the time they found him, the healers couldn't help."

"That's why Malfina isn't working as much," Zori explained. "She actually stopped working at all for a while. Her grief clouds her vision, so she only sees when she's in a better mood. She has an assistant book her clients' requirements, then does her work when she can, so if you go to her shop, you'll probably find her assistant there instead of her."

I nodded. I wasn't sure I was ready to hear about the vision, but if I changed my mind, maybe I'd see Martha at Mystic Mugs again or riding around in a pedicab.

"I heard she secretly hated her son," Shea said, releasing my neck to lean on her cane.

Azura lightly smacked Shea's arm. "See? This is why I don't like gossip. People will talk about anything, no matter how cruel." She smiled at me. "We can be there if you talk to Madam Malfina, if you want. Just let us know."

I forced down the lump in my throat. "Thanks. I'm not sure I'm ready for that, though. My brain can only process so much."

"That's understandable," Lacey said. "If you ever want to talk about your mom, I'm here."

With a nod, I released her hand. "I appreciate that."

She continued to bag my purchases.

"Can your brain handle our magic lesson?" Zori asked. "We can cancel."

Sylvie had insisted I start learning to control my magic, and I agreed. Even though I hadn't had another outburst, I grew more curious about magic each day. "I promised you and Sylvie dinner in exchange for a lesson, and I will follow through. Plus, I *really* want a wand."

Zori pumped her fist...right into a cluster of necklaces floating by. Shea shifted into a raven to help undo the tangle Zori created. I just chuckled and paid Lacey, thanking her for helping me.

On the way to the door, Sunset and Twilight stopped at a carousel of suspended scarves in a variety of colors and textures, their little eyes wide.

"Kinley..." Twilight's eyes had locked onto a yellow plaid scarf.

I ran my fingers over the fabric before letting them fall onto the next scarf over—a thick fuchsia design perfect for winter. Lacey stood a few feet away watching me with a knowing look. "Do these fit to the wearer's size too?" I asked.

Twilight's new kitty-sized scarves soared behind her neck as I rode us home on my grandmother's bicycle, and I could just see the tips of Sunset's new turquoise scarf poking out of Zori's pack as she flew overhead.

Chapter Eighteen

"**A** proper witch needs a proper wand."

Sylvie reached into her backpack and pulled out an oak wand that looked like Dusk had used it as a chew toy on multiple occasions. She whisked it through the air. The remnants of our dinner from Ilusionista, a restaurant that served amazing pupusas—stuffed corn-meal cakes cooked on a griddle—and other cuisine from El Salvador, swept themselves into the kitchen trash can.

She held the wand out to me, and I tried to figure out the best place to grab it without getting a splinter. I finally reached out two fingers to pinch the end when she pulled it back, her bark of laughter filling the long kitchen. "Oh, Kinley, your face."

Zori held up her phone screen. "I took a picture."

I snorted. "I'll happily use that half-masticated wand. Splinters may invade my fingers, but I'll get over it. I just want to learn."

Twilight lifted her head from the snugglefest of familiars happening on the island behind us. "Kinley, that wand is toe-up. You cannot use it. Your stock would plummet."

"Did they only have one movie where you're from?" I asked, recognizing her words from her favorite film. "We need to start expanding your Hollywood horizons beyond *Clueless*."

Her ears flattened and her eyes shone in the dim light. "I'd love that."

I smiled at the goofy cat and turned back to the witches at the table. Sylvie reached into her backpack and pulled out a long, unadorned purple box. As I took in its shape, sweeping cursive words wrote themselves across the matte paint: Wicked Witch Wands.

Zori nudged me with her elbow. "Go on."

The words had transfixed me so much that I hadn't realized Sylvie was waiting for me to take the box.

"Sylvie, I can't—"

"Yes, you can."

As if they could hear her, Twilight whispered, "Take it. Don't offend her."

I lifted it from Sylvie's hands, set it on the table, and watched the words vanish and form one more time before opening the lid. A thin, gorgeous wand with a violet handle rested on a plump white cushion. It blurred as tears obscured my vision.

Of course. I knew as soon as I saw the box that Sylvie had gone back for the wand I'd longed for that first day I'd arrived on Sea Sprite Isle.

With a slight shake to my hand, I reached out to graze my fingertips over the ivory wand body, covered in black, typed words. I read a few lines, and the tears finally spilled down my cheeks. The book pages encircling the shaft appeared to come from *Lost in Sea Sprite Wood*, the same book whose cover occupied the bathroom door upstairs.

A jumble of emotions choked me. Gratitude. Joy. Sadness. I forced myself to speak. "Sylvie, thank you so much. No one has given me anything so thoughtful in decades. Not since my first foster family, the Huberts, passed away."

Zori leaned over to wrap an arm around my shoulders, her head coming to rest against mine.

Sylvie reached up to tug on the headphones she always wore around her neck. "You are so welcome. I knew you had to have it. I'm sorry the people around you haven't given you anything special."

I shrugged. "I'm realizing it's partially my fault. After the Huberts passed, I pulled back from people. The pain overwhelmed me, and I didn't want to go through that again. Didn't want to lose anyone else. I kept that up for a long time." I dug my thumbnail into the tip of my pinky. "When I finally sought connections, I subconsciously looked for superficial people who wouldn't really care. I attached to emotionally detached people. Not to say they weren't responsible too. They were."

"Well, you have us now," Zori said, squeezing me.

"We're here for you." Sylvie came over to hug us from behind. "For whatever you need, including to learn magic."

"Right." I wiped my eyes. "Let's do this."

We broke apart, and the witches had me stand on the far side of the kitchen table with my back to the French doors that led to the backyard. Twilight, Dusk, and Sunset sat up on the island, watching intently.

Sylvie set a penny in front of me, the copper dulled by years of grime. "We're starting with a simple cleaning spell."

Zori slid the wand box to me. "Go ahead. Pick it up."

I bit my lip. "What if I blow up the kitchen? This house has survived for so long, and then *bam*, I come along and explode it."

Sylvie pulled out her own wand and said a few Latin words. A warm bubble formed around us. "Protection spell," she explained. "Now you can't hurt anything."

"Even if you did," Zori said, coming to stand beside me, "we could fix it with magic."

Of course. Just like Ryland did to my bridal suite. Feeling reassured, I picked up the wand. When the kitchen utensils didn't embed themselves into the walls and the doors behind me didn't blow off their hinges, I took that as a good sign.

The wand felt light, like holding a piece of pipe cleaner. "So, what do I do?"

Zori and Sylvie took out their own coins before demonstrating a complicated maneuver with their wands and saying, "Lavitum!"

Both pennies turned the shiny and brilliant copper of their youths.

That looked easy. I could do that.

Ten minutes later, they hadn't even let me mutter the spell.

"You're doing a little whirl with the wand instead of a twirl," Zori told me.

I gaped at her. "Those sound like the same thing."

"No, no. Watch."

She showed me for the eighty-fourth time. I tried again, and she clapped. "Yes! That's it!"

Sylvie smiled and pointed to the coin. "You're ready. Add the spell. Just one word: Lavitum. Make sure to draw on your power. The wand will focus it, but you need to pull from your well of power actively for it to work."

I nodded. Page had explained this to me. That pink pool of my magic I'd found while bonding with him was always available to me. I just had to set my intention to it.

Closing my eyes, I connected with the eager magic waiting under my skin. Then I took a breath and lifted my lids, focusing on the dirty penny. I whisked and flicked and swooshed my wand, and as I moved into the last arc, I shouted, "Lavitum!"

A stream of rose-pink magic shot out of my wand—right at the familiars on the island in front of us.

I sucked in a breath as the spell hit them, sure I'd killed them all, but the spell expanded to cover them. I could see little bristles rake through their fur for several seconds before the magic dissipated.

The cat, raccoon, and red panda stared at me with matching expressions of horror.

"I'm WET!" Twilight yelled.

She wasn't just wet. Every soaked piece of her fur stood on end like she'd been electrocuted, as did that of her familiar friends' fur.

Zori clapped a hand to her mouth, her shoulders shaking. Sylvie took out her phone to snap a few shots.

"You did the wand twirl again," Zori told me, pulling her hand away from her mouth just a bit.

"And you got so excited to say the spell, you raised your wand," Sylvie explained. "That spell isn't meant for living beings."

Twilight stomped a foot. "This is so not the makeover I wanted, Kinley!"

A petulant, puffed-up cat was enough to break through my shock, and I had to cough to cover up my rising laughter.

Dusk started frantically flattening her fur with her human-like hands. But the fur just stood back up. She flashed Sylvie a venomous look when she started guffawing. The expression was so ridiculous on her little raccoon face that I lost it too. Zori joined us, and soon we had tears on our cheeks and angry familiars shaking fists and paws at us.

"Okay, that's enough," Zori declared after Sunset kicked her bag off the counter. "Sorry, familiars." She raised her wand and performed a grooming spell which fixed their fur. Then she circled them, gathering air from the room to blast the animals until they dried.

Sylvie directed me back to the penny. "Time to try again."

Three sets of paws skittered across the counter, down the far side of the island, and out of the kitchen.

"That's probably for the best," I said.

After thirty minutes half-filled with me moving my wand wrong and half-filled with me grousing about how I'd never memorize such complicated wand movements, a sprinkle of pink magic hit the coin and restored it to mint condition.

I jumped up and down. "I did it."

"I knew you could do it, Kinley." Sylvie clapped and gave me a little bow.

"Hex, yeah!" Zori grabbed my hand and spun me in a circle.

Warmth suffused my chest and laughter bubbled from me as my friend released me. My shoes kept moving, and I let the momentum carry me across the kitchen, flinging my wand arm out when I finally came to a stop, as if I expected someone to yell, "Ta da!"

Instead, a loud burst of shattering glass and yelping familiars filled the house.

My lungs seized. What had I done? I'd danced right out of the protection spell and flung my wand out without thinking.

"Sunset!" Zori shouted, echoed by Sylvie's call to her familiar.

I turned to run for the front of the house, yelling for Twilight like my fellow witches. Mark plastered himself to the glass as I passed the atrium. I'd have to reassure the semi-sentient sunflower later.

Relief had me clutching my chest when Twilight called back, "Wow! That was exciting. Like being in a James Bond movie. Kinley, can we watch the Bond movies first?"

She was okay.

Sunset and Dusk did not look as thrilled as my familiar when I rounded the corner into the living room. The three fur babies sat on the blue sofa, covered in tiny shards of glass from the obliterated front window.

"Don't move!" I told them.

Sunset gave me an "obviously" look.

Zori and Sylvie skidded into the room.

Sylvie put her hands on her head. "Hexes, they're okay."

"Are any of you cut?" Zori asked, and my heart broke when Dusk held up a paw with a tiny bubble of blood on it. "Just a few seconds, and we'll clean that up." Zori lifted her hands, manipulating the surrounding air to lift all the glass. She collapsed it into a pile on the floor by the window.

Sylvie went over to inspect Dusk's paw before muttering a spell. Then she kissed Dusk's nose.

"I'm so sorry," I said, tugging on my braid. "I can't believe I hurt you, Dusk."

Everyone looked at me, but Twilight spoke first.

"You didn't do this, Kinley. A massive, spelled rock crashed through the window."

I dropped my braid. "What?"

She lifted a paw and pointed just beyond the coffee table.

"Twilight says a rock broke the window." I stepped over to find a thick, eight-inch-long rock with a four-letter word carved into it:

STOP

Huh? I bent to pick it up, but Sylvie sent a lasso of magic at my arm. "Don't! It could be dangerous."

I reared back, and Sylvie's magic dissipated. Breathing hard, I looked at the shattered bay window before turning to the other five beings in the room. "The rock says 'stop.' That's it."

Zori ran a hand through her waves. "Someone's noticed."

"Noticed?" I asked.

"That we're investigating, Kinley. The killer knows."

A stab of anger hit me. The killer dropped Denise on my porch, and now they threaten me and hurt Dusk? "Oh, spell no."

Sylvie pulled out her phone. "I'll call Ryland."

I rushed over and put my hand over her phone. "No!"

She tensed. "Kinley, the MBI needs to know about this."

"We know things the MBI doesn't. If we tell Ryland about this, he'll make us stop investigating, and those things might never come to light. The killer could get away with killing Denise."

Zori came to my side. "I agree, Sylvie. We must be on the right track. I know Detective Fores is like a nephew to you, so we're asking a lot, but...please?" She put her hands under either side of her chin.

Back and forth, Sylvie's eyes moved, from me to Zori, before her shoulders finally relaxed. "Fine, but just this once. You have to promise that if the killer makes any other threats, you'll tell Ryland."

I crossed my heart. "Promise."

Both women's brows furrowed. "What was that?"

"What, this?" I crossed my heart again.

They nodded.

"You know, cross my heart and hope to die?" Blank looks. "I take it magical folks don't say that when they make a promise."

Zori chuckled. "No, we don't include death in our promises. Witches say, 'By the maiden, the mother, and the crone, to this I will hold.'"

"Okay." I looked at Sylvie. "What she said."

With a nod, Sylvie exchanged her phone for her wand and turned to the window. With two quick swishes and a few words I didn't catch, the glass shot back into the window.

I popped a hip out. "Thank you for doing that, but one question. Why did that spell have such an easy wand movement compared to the cleaning spell?"

Zori and Sylvie exchanged amused glances.

"The cleaning spell isn't as easy as we led you to believe," Sylvie said. "We wanted you to see how complicated the wand work can be, so you know to practice. The actual *magic* is quite easy and doesn't take much out of you, though, so it made for a good first spell."

I rubbed my temples. "That makes sense, I suppose."

"Now, let's look at this rock." Zori wove through the furniture to get to the rock. She and Sylvie proceeded to examine it for ten minutes, finally concluding that it didn't have any more magic attached to it. They levitated it into a closet for me before gathering their backpacks and familiars. Dusk watched with covetous eyes as Zori tied Sunset's scarf around his neck.

Zori gave me one last wave from the yard before she climbed onto her broom and shot into the sky with Sunset on her back. Sylvie and Dusk took off a moment later.

"Dusk wants a scarf too," Twilight said from where she sat by my feet on the porch.

I lifted her into my arms. "You're such a trendsetter."

Her ears twitched. "Maybe I need an indoor scarf too. Oh! What about a necklace?"

"Maybe. Let's solve the murder first."

"Yeah, we need to show this murderer they can't mess with us. It's too bad I didn't see them, or I would have gouged my claws into their eyes and their mouth and—"

"Yep, I get it." I carried her inside and shut the door. "We must have found something important or the killer wouldn't have threatened us. I have a plan, but it's been a long day, so let's get some sleep. I'll carry you to your room."

Twilight looked up at me. "Maybe I better sleep with you tonight. You know, for your protection. In case the killer comes back. You might need me."

I kissed her nose. "Mm hmm. Totally. *I* might need *you.* Just no sleeping on my head. Your snores are otherworldly. I need to find some earplugs."

Chapter Nineteen

"Oat milk latte with a focus elixir." Zori beamed at me as she set my order on Mystic Mug's counter.

I pushed my migraine glasses up my nose and grabbed the cup. My latte had full caffeine this morning. The pink lenses were precautionary, due to the sun's overwhelming presence this morning. While the light bothered me, my head hadn't started to ache too much yet.

"Where's mine?" Twilight asked, shaking her head so her yellow plaid scarf swayed. Then she looked around to see if the other familiars in the shop had noticed. Twilight had awoken that morning with a declaration on her scratchy tongue: she'd be wearing the scarf indoors and outdoors, all day.

Zori laughed and set a tiny cup of whipped cream down for Twilight, who immediately shoved her face in it.

"So, you have a plan?" Zori asked. Despite the hour—close to eight a.m.—the line had died down, so my friend leaned over the counter, knocking over a pile of extra lids.

I nodded. "We'll see how much time I have today since we're opening the bookshop for a while." At that thought, my stomach flipped over and tried to expel my oatmeal. "But we obviously know something important, probably something the police don't know—or the killer wouldn't bother to threaten us. It must have to do with Denise's shady—"

"Oh, Denise was shady," a high voice said.

A twenty-something brunette in orange running shorts and a tight tank top reached around me to grab a straw, and I mentally slapped myself for talking about the investigation in the open.

"Sorry, I dropped my straw, and I couldn't help but overhear you as I walked up here." The woman tucked back a loose strand of her ponytail, looking a bit awkward, like she might run away without finishing her thought.

"Don't apologize!" If she knew something about Denise, I wanted to hear it. I tilted my head and flashed a smile. "Denise really was *shifty*."

"Yeah, I always thought so," Zori said. "Do you know something, Georgina?"

Of course, Zori knew her. Thank you, small towns.

Georgina nodded and dropped her voice to an excited whisper. "I saw her talking to these two really *questionable* guys when I went for my morning run. I don't usually judge people by their appearance. They were dirty and shabby looking, but so are a lot of folks when they finish fishing. It wasn't that. The way they moved and their eyes...the two clearly had taken Intimidation 101. They were towering over Denise, trying to make her feel small."

"Ha," Zori said. "I bet that went over really well with Denise."

"Just like you'd imagine. She puffed herself up like a dragon and let them have it."

My hand tightened on my cup and the lid popped off. "What did she say?"

Georgina shook her head. "I don't know. The wind carried their voices away from me."

Hexes. "When did you see this?"

She tapped the unopened straw on her leg. "Maybe two months ago?"

Recently enough for me to count these guys as suspects. "Can you describe the men?"

"Both were white and tall. One had long, dirty-blond hair—the color and the cleanliness—pulled into a ponytail. He had a patchy beard too. The other had dark brown or black hair just above his shoulders. Scraggly, shaggy hair. That's all I remember."

"Do you know where you saw them?" Zori asked.

Georgina pointed to the far side of the shop. "Foxglove Point."

I guess Foxglove Point was that way.

"Thanks, Georgina. Your next latte is on me," Zori said with a wink.

After throwing my barista pal a coy smile, Georgina crossed to a small table, inserted her straw into an iced latte, picked it up, and left the shop...with Zori watching the whole time.

I caught sight of Madam Malfina at the neighboring table, and she gave me a friendly wave. This would be the perfect time to ask her about the vision she had about me and my parents, but my feet went numb at the thought. I didn't feel ready to unravel the mystery around my parents yet. I'd stick with Denise's murder.

Twilight, having finally come up for air from her whipped cream cup, trilled and pranced around on the counter. "Zori has a crush."

"I agree, Twilight. Zori does have a crush."

With pink cheeks, Zori waved me off. "Naw, I just think she's nice. I'm not ready to date right now. Bad breakup with my ex-boyfriend. And a bad breakup with my ex-girl-friend before that."

I lifted my cup. "To not dating after bad breakups. Who needs love?"

She giggled and held up an invisible cup. "Hear, hear!"

A crowd of people and animals entered. Several of the animals turned into people, and they all got in line. Zori rushed off to make drinks.

Grabbing Twilight, I said, "Let's go open the bookshop for the first time."

My nerves tingled as I turned, feeling unsure if I could do this with just me, a cat, and a sentient bookshop on my side. But I found a ghost in a bowler hat waiting for me with a luminous smile on her transparent face.

"Oh! Tansy!" I said while Twilight meowed at her.

She tipped her hat. "I wouldn't miss Margaret's grand-daughter's grand reopening of The Perfect Page for anything. Ready to become a bookseller?"

"Why is no one coming inside?"

The stab of disappointment in my gut took me by surprise. When I'd unlocked the doors and turned the sign to open, I'd been praying for no customers. I didn't feel ready. Page had only trained me for a few days. I'd never sold a book in my life. My magic still felt new and untested.

But now that the store had been empty for an hour, I felt upset. If not for me, then for Page. He'd missed providing customers with the books their souls required. Months had passed without his unique ability—his *purpose*—having a use.

"It's raining, but that's normal for Oregon," I added to Page, Tansy, and Twilight, the latter of whom sat on the marble counter swishing her tail. The earlier sunshine had vanished behind a row of stampeding clouds.

Page's rumbling voice wrapped around me. *We haven't spread the word outside, or even inside, of town that we're open, so only passersby know.*

Twilight put a paw on my clenched hand. "And also everyone thinks you're a murderer, Kinley."

I snorted and repeated the cat's words for Tansy while a melody of fluttering pages played in my mind as Page chuckled.

"Twilight, not everyone thinks Kinley is a murderer," Tansy said, playing with her necktie. "Just...many of them. I'm sure we'll get a customer soon."

I tugged on the cuffs of my new green blouse patterned with tiny gold unicorns moving across the fabric. It was a special day, and I'd wanted to look fancy. Too bad no one had come in to see my whimsical top. "Well, at least with no customers we have time to start over on the case. To look at everything." I flicked my eyes to the rafters. "Do we have a whiteboard, markers, and a printer?"

Yes, Page said.

My familiar cocked her head. "Wait, this is your plan? To *look* at everything?"

I gave her a confident nod. "Yes. We know something that has the killer scared. Let's figure out what."

Twenty minutes later, I had all the suspects mapped out and all the information I knew listed on the whiteboard that Page had pulled from *somewhere* and moved to the stockroom. Page had assured me three times that, if a customer entered, he'd let me know asap.

"One last thing to add before we print some photos," I said, jogging to my tote bag in the office and returning with a piece of stationery covered in loopy, scarlet letters.

"What is that?" Tansy asked.

Smoothing the creases, I said, "A threatening note Denise received. I took it from her house."

Tansy put her hands on her hips. "Kinley! You stole *evidence*?"

I bit my lip. "Technically, yes, but my magic told me to take it." Even now, it tingled at my touch.

Twilight spun in a circle at our feet. "You're so bad, Kinley. I like this side of you."

Page's displeasure creaked like a book spine that hadn't been cracked in decades. *Kinley...*

"Yes?" I winced, ready for him to chastise me.

You've had this since the night before last and didn't bring it to me immediately?

That was what Page cared about? Not that I pilfered it? "Should I have? When we left Denise's secret room, everyone thought the letter got put back, but something about it called to me, so I kept it. I figured my magic wanted me to look at it more, but I looked at it again that night and last night. Nothing new got my attention."

Page sighed and the paper I held actually fluttered, like he'd breathed directly on it. *You are an untrained bibliowitch. It makes sense you didn't find anything. The secrets of books and their derivatives—ink, paper, etc.—take time to understand. I can help you. Any other book-related items you've been hiding?*

I shrugged. "I don't think so."

Twilight batted her paws on my boot. "Kinley, don't forget the record books from Denise's shop."

"Sure, but I didn't steal those. Shea took pictures. She sent them to me, and I was going to print them and look them over, but that can't be the same as holding the actual book."

Hmm. You're correct, but we can look anyway, Page said.

Tansy leaned in. "Can you update me on your conversation?"

"Oh! Sorry."

After I'd caught her up, we printed the photos of the three record books Denise kept in her desk.

We all agreed that the red ledger, which showed her normal customer sales data, didn't hold anything of interest to us. Page and Tansy puzzled over the photos from the second book for a while, examining the red and black rows tracking amounts owed and paid with only two designations between the rows: BTLY and DSKT. They admitted defeat, and we moved on.

I taped up the last photos of the book with rows written in light gray ink, which held two columns of coded data and one column with dollar amounts.

Twilight tilted her head. "I still don't know why you took those pictures."

Waving my arm at the whiteboard, I said, "I took photos so we could do this."

Tansy floated over to look at the last set of pictures. "Yes, but why capture images of this book? The others are useful, but why this one?"

I looked between Twilight and Tansy. "This book could have something helpful too."

Page's chortle vibrated through me. *Kinley, I believe Denise wrote that book in invisible ink. Only you and I can see it.*

Twilight bounced on her paws. "No way! That's so cool."

"These pages look blank to you?" I asked Tansy.

"Umm, yes?"

I ran my fingers through my loose hair. We had found invisible ink at Denise's house. "Apparently, the ink is invisible. Unless you're a bibliowitch or bibliobookshop." I described the columns to Tansy and Twilight. "Denise likely wrote her nefarious transactions here. Wouldn't the cops easily figure this out, though? Even humans have invisible ink."

"Denise was a very good enchanter," Tansy said. "It's possible this ink wouldn't have even set off a magic detector, given her skill level. If the MBI's magic detectors did go off, they would have tested the book further, but they'd need another strong enchanter or a bibliowitch to reveal the ink. The MBI has a lot of resources, so they might have found someone."

"Even if they did, they'd need to figure out what the data means," I said.

Speaking of, Page rumbled. *The left column has frequently repeated codes, and the prices often repeat within those codes. I believe those codes must refer to the item Denise sold.*

I looked at the left column and explained Page's theory to Tansy. Then I wrote down all the ledger entries going six months back so Twilight and Tansy could read it too.

Twilight jumped onto my shoulder to see better. "CS, HM, CM, PS, and EP. Those are all the codes I see."

My mind whirred through all the offerings I knew Denise had. "She had a piece of poisoned stationery in the hidden room at her house. Maybe she coded those orders as PS."

"You said she had cursed stationery too. Maybe that's CS," Twilight said.

I wrote down our ideas. We kept brainstorming until we'd decided HM might be for a hidden message with invisible ink, CM for compulsion message, and EP for the exam pens.

"Great, now let's focus on the second column full of random letters and numbers," Tansy said.

We all looked at the codes, which ranged from three to seven digits, for twenty minutes, with Twilight making increasingly ridiculous suggestions about their meanings, the final being a government conspiracy about cursed trees and their paper products causing warts. None of us had any response to that except to move on.

I picked up the letter Denise had received that threatened revenge against her for cursing the sender's sister. I let my fingers graze over the red words. No doubt the color had been chosen to intimidate. "Everyone was worried this paper might curse us, but I knew it wouldn't."

Ah, yes, your magic's intuition, Page said. *I think you'll be able to glean much more from it now. Perhaps even identify who wrote it.*

My eyebrows pinched together. "Could Denise have identified the sender? If she didn't already know?"

No. Denise's skills with ink and paper came from her primary magic as an enchanter. Yours come from bibliomancy: Perceiving books, paper, and ink in their present state and their past state. The second half of the word, 'mancy,' refers to divination in general. The way I can see into someone's soul to know which book they need at that moment is a form of divination. The way you can read ink, paper, and books for their secrets and their histories is a form of divination as well.

"Divination?" I asked, feeling like the words on the pages of my mind had been scrambled *once again* this week.

Don't overthink it. For now, you just have to read that paper. You simply need to relax into your magic.

Putting one hand on each side of the paper, I closed my eyes and found my magic. The peony-pink pool felt cheerful, welcoming, and just a bit warm, like a cup of tea left to cool to the perfect temperature. I let my mind's fingers glide under the surface for a few moments before simply resting my hand inside the magic.

Now what? I asked Page with my thoughts.

Feel the letter in your hands on the physical plane.

I let myself feel the paper. It warmed at my touch, each letter prickling at my skin.

Now, allow a visual of the letter to enter your mind, Page continued.

The scarlet ink sprang right into my brain. I could see every pen stroke:

Denise,

If I could have cursed this letter like you cursed my sister, I would have. But I'll have my revenge. One day, when you're walking in those ugly shoes, thinking about which cookie you might have that night, I'll come out of nowhere. You'll never see me, never hear me coming.

-T

Does anything stand out? Page asked.

One by one, I let my magic drape over the words, encapsulating each in its glow. The last letter, T, glimmered brighter than the others.

The signature, I said.

Good, Page told me. *That makes sense. The sender's initial would have the strongest connection to them. Focus on it.*

I let the other letters fall away and pushed all my magic into the T. It flushed to a smoldering neon pink before the lines swelled, growing to something I couldn't contain, until finally, they burst and the rest of the signature flowed out in those same loopy letters: Twistie Wistie.

With a gasp, I released my magic and dropped the letter.

Breathe, Kinley, Page said. *Tremendous job.*

After a few rounds of breathing, I opened my eyes to find Twilight's face right in mine. I grabbed my heart. "Hexes. I forgot you'd jumped onto my shoulder."

"Are you okay? What happened?"

I lifted her and tucked her against my side. "I'm fine."

Tansy adjusted her hat. "Did you learn anything?"

"I got the rest of the sender's name. It's weird though. Twistie Wistie."

"Huh." Tansy scrunched her nose. "We don't have anyone in town with that name. That wouldn't be a fun name to grow up with."

Twilight wriggled around. "It's gotta be a nickname."

Page's *Hmm* reverberated through me. *A woman named Wisteria uses the name Twistie Wistie in her online persona. A resident of Meadowsweet, she uses social media to promote her broomstick riding skills. Her CharmChat videos have a lot of views. You can find her under the username @twistiewistie95.*

Something tickled my brain at that username. I let it spin in my brain for a minute before I snapped my fingers. "I knew that sounded familiar. @twistiewistie95 left a comment for Denise telling her to 'go shave your head, you fleabag.' I thought they were just a random internet troll, but they were trolling her in real life too."

Tansy tapped on—or rather, *through*—the whiteboard. "T-W-9-5."

I jerked my head around to look at the board, wincing as my neck muscles tightened. Tansy's transparent finger hovered above the column of seemingly random letters and numbers in Denise's secret ledger. Alongside TW95 was the code CS and a hefty sum of money. Twistie Wistie was Denise's customer.

Twilight's claws dug into my skin. "Do you think the other entries could refer to social media names?"

I tugged on a lock of hair. "Maybe? We won't know unless we find more customers."

Did you not already interrogate another in the kitchen? Page asked.

"Oh! Tyler. He showed us his CharmChat account to prove his alibi. I remember it because it was cute: bigtylerlovesyou. B-T-L-Y."

Twilight purred. "Aww, how sweet!"

A feeling of ineptitude washed over me as I immediately remembered those four letters from Denise's other ledger with red and black rows, tracking amounts owed and paid for the two codes BTLY and DSKT. I'd known Tyler's social media handle for days and hadn't put the pieces together.

I pointed to those photos. "Denise logged a lot of money from BTLY—Tyler—in this ledger. There's only one other person she tracked payments from in here. Why?"

"Probably because she could rely on those payments on a regular basis," Tansy said. "Because she was blackmailing Tyler into selling the pens with the exam answers."

"Which means," I said with a sigh, "she was probably blackmailing the other person too. So whoever DSKT is, they had a motive to kill Denise."

"We'd need a high-powered algorithm to find all the usernames on magical social media that fit the DSKT initials," Tansy said.

I blew out a breath. "So we focus on Twistie Wistie, who we know threatened Denise."

I've watched the last twenty of her videos, Page said.

Wow, he was fast.

She appears to fly in the same location in Meadowsweet most nights. I believe it's near the college.

Twilight rubbed her head on my shirt, and the little unicorns fled, rushing away across the fabric. "Kinley! Does that mean we get to go to Meadowsweet?"

I nodded. "Yes. After we sell some books." Now that we had a new suspect, I felt energized and ready to get Page some customers.

We poked our heads back out front. The rain had let up, so I asked Page if we had an A-frame sign and some chalk. My art skills could use some serious magical assistance, but I cobbled together a message and put the board outside.

Now Open.

(And I'm Not A Murderer.)

Chapter Twenty

"**I**nteresting sign. Though, perhaps not very family-oriented."

I looked up from where I'd been posting a photo of Twilight in her scarf to the shop's CharmChat to find a woman in her mid-forties with bronze skin and wearing a black hijab giving me a mildly chastising but still rather bemused look.

"Mayor Adel!" Tansy said, passing through the counter. "Is the sign too much?"

"No way, the sign is perfect," Twilight protested for only my and Page's ears.

The mayor put her hands on her slight hips. "Tansy, I've told you a thousand times to call me Rehema." She winked at me with one of her keen russet-brown eyes, so I supposed I wasn't in too much trouble for the sign. "You too."

"Oh, umm, thanks. I'm Kinley." I set my phone down and held my hand out.

She shook it, her grip tight. "It's lovely to meet you." Twilight trotted over and held her paw out. The mayor took it next. "And you are?"

"That's Twilight," I said.

"Nice to make your acquaintance, Twilight. Your scarf is gorgeous." Twilight meowed and rubbed her head on Rehema's purple sleeve. The mayor looked up at me. "I adored your grandmother."

I smiled. "That seems to be a theme. Well, except for..." My eyes flicked to the ceiling.

"Ah, yes, Denise. She didn't like anyone, and the feeling was mutual. I highly doubt you murdered her, but the sign feels like a little much. How about we make a deal? You change it to 'criminal' instead of 'murderer,' and I'll spread the word around town that The Perfect Page has opened again, and that I shopped here without being choked to death."

"Oh, that's much better," Tansy said, pulling on the sides of her wide-legged pants. "That won't scare any children."

"Boo," Twilight protested. "That's boring. Murderer has more pizazz."

A laugh bubbled up my throat. "Twi, I've had enough pizazz this week for a lifetime." I patted her head before telling the mayor, "I'll take your deal. Thank you for helping us."

"Of course!" She rubbed her hands together. "Okay, now for the real reason I came here. Page, I've been in a reading slump without you. Please, find me a good book."

Here we go, Kinley, Page said. *First customer. Are you ready?*

"Let's do this," I said.

I led her down the counter to the end opposite the cash register. Two gold circles appeared on the white marble, lit by Page's magic. "Place your hands in the circles," I said, but Rehema had already begun reaching for them. Not her first rodeo, then. Or should I say *readeo*?

When the mayor's hands touched the marble, the gold light engulfed her hands. Ten seconds later, a hardback book flew through the stacks and stopped inches from her face.

"Ooooh!" She snagged the book. "*The Wolf Viking's Fake Fairy Bride.*"

Wow. Did Page really just send the mayor a book about a fake engagement between a fairy and a Viking wolf shifter? Rehema flipped the book around to show me the cover. Between the fur, the wings, the axe, and the abs, I concluded, yes.

"Kinleeeey," Twilight said. "We need to read that." I ignored her...but decided to inspect the book later. Only to satisfy my bookseller interest, of course.

"Thanks, Page." Rehema gave a thumbs-up to a random bookshelf. "I can't wait to read it." Then she did something terrifying. She asked me, "Do you have any recommendations?"

I just stared at her for a few seconds until Tansy elbowed me, her incorporeal limb passing right through. "Umm."

I needed to be better prepared for that question. Page had told me that not everyone wanted him to find the book their soul needed. Some customers didn't want that much insight into their soul. Some didn't want a mysterious sentient bookshop accessing their soul. Others just felt a bit creeped out by it.

None of them realized that Page didn't need them to put their hands in the gold circles to read their soul. He could read them the second they stepped inside. But, again, that creeped out customers, so the Paigewrights had led customers to believe they had to put their hands in the circles for Page to read them.

If they opted out, they could browse the shop, but they might want to ask the resident bibliowitch for recommendations instead. I couldn't read their soul like Page could, but I could glean a certain understanding of a customer's tastes.

Which is how I knew to lead Rehema to the mystery section. Letting my magic talk to me, I dusted my fingers along the spines. The books sighed in pleasure. "You like lighthearted mysteries, I believe?"

The mayor nodded. "Yes."

"With a bit of romance?"

"Right again."

I paused in front of a case full of cozy mysteries, aware of Tansy and Twilight giving me encouraging looks from ten feet to my left. My fingers inspected the books, a slight buzz informing me when I'd touched something Rehema might like. I kept going until I felt a stronger zing. When I inspected the book, I snickered.

Rehema accepted the paperback with a glint in her eye. "I've heard of this one. A mystery about a witch who has to clear her name of murder with the help of her gray cat and her ornery uncle."

Twilight spun in a circle. "A gray cat? We have to read that!" I had a feeling Twilight would want to read all the books.

Rehema swept her eyes across the store. "Hmm, an ornery uncle. That sounds like someone we know, doesn't it?"

A nearby set of wingback chairs and a chess table that sat between them rattled, but none of the pieces fell.

The mayor laughed loud enough to drown out the rattling. "See, Page? You're ornery."

I could just barely see the front door fly open. A second later, a paper bag with the store's logo came flying over to us. Both the mayor's books left her hands and landed in the bag.

"I think Page wants me to go," Rehema said, sounding positively delighted about it.

"C'mon," I said. "I'll ring you up. That is, if you want the mystery book?"

She clutched the bag to her chest. "Absolutely."

As I passed Tansy, she held her hand up for a high-five. As our hands passed through each other, I mouthed, "I did it!"

Chapter Twenty-One

"**M**oon and mandrake! My first portal!" Twilight made figure eights around my legs, her body a gray and yellow blur.

"Ryland took us through a portal to my condo just a couple days ago, you goofy cat."

She paused and glanced up at me with wide pupils. "Kinley, this is *nothing* like that."

I'd gathered as much. For one, Ryland's portal hadn't needed me to have a shiny ID with a surprisingly great photo of me that hadn't even required a retina-burning flash to capture. Tansy had taken me to the town hall to get the ID when we'd closed down the shop after a successful first day with dozens of customers who apparently just needed to be assured I wasn't a criminal.

Ryland's portals also involved simply stepping—or being tackled—through, not getting in a frickin' mint-green *train car*.

I zipped up my black jacket against the growing nip in the air as my eyes explored the portal site from our location by a back wall covered in ivory subway tiles.

Three lines roped in by glowing lemon-yellow magic led to enchanted check-in stands. Signs above each line declared them to serve travelers headed to Meadowsweet, Hollyhock, and Magicville—because I guess even magical beings got lazy with names.

Every few minutes, travelers in one line would move forward, passing through an archway to a platform I couldn't see much of—just a small glance of the trains as they pulled in and out of the station.

"Kinley!" Zori came jogging up to me, still wearing her goggles and holding her curlicue broom. Sunset peeked over her shoulder, his scarf knotted around his neck. "Ready to ride?"

I pointed to her broom. "Not that thing."

She laughed and collapsed her broom. "*The train.*"

Twilight bounced on her toes. "I am!"

"My familiar is more than ready. Why do they need the train? Why not just let people go through the portal a few at a time?"

She pushed her goggles up. "It's dangerous. We can't have anyone getting lost to the ether, can we?"

I felt my brow furrow.

"If you cross with a portal witch, they can guide you, but we don't have enough portal witches to guide each person wanting to cross every portal, all day. That would exhaust them. Not only that, but it would prevent them from doing other work. If Detective Fores had to be here, he couldn't do his MBI work. Portal witches create and sustain these portals, but they aren't here all day. The trains are part of the magic. They guide us through so no one gets lost to the nothingness in between places."

"Gotcha."

A raven soared through the open-air entrance to the station and shifted into Shea. She shook herself off in a way that reminded me of a bird ruffling its feathers. Tugging down the hem of her long emerald coat, she said, "I thought I might not make it in time. Someone left a litter of puppies outside the shelter's back door. I had to find a volunteer to check them in before I could go."

Twilight climbed up Shea's jeans until my friend picked her up. "Puppies? You have puppies? Can I play with them?"

I chuckled. "Twilight wants to play with the puppies."

Shea booped her nose. "Maybe once they have all their shots."

"I'm so sorry!" Azura hurried over to us, her wings waving behind her, leaving a trail of golden shimmer. "I'm never late."

Shea looked at her phone and put the back of her hand on her forehead. "You're one minute late! The entire night is ruined. Let's give up on this murder suspect. Just go home, Azura. Go home to Birch. You must be sick. They can make you soup and—"

Azura smacked her on the arm before turning to me. "I don't like being late. Shea thinks I take myself too seriously."

I smiled. "I've been known to do that too." Shea and Zori led us to the line marked Meadowsweet. "Who's Birch?" I asked.

She pushed her braids behind her shoulders and dug into her purse to extract her ID. "My fiancé. I'm sure you'll meet them soon."

I braced myself for the impact that word—fiancé—would have on me, but I let out a relieved breath when it felt more like being smacked by one of Twilight's paws than being socked by a heavyweight champ. "Congratulations," I said, squeezing her arm.

"Thank—oh, Kinley, sorry." Her purple-dusted eyes scrunched as she winced.

"Don't apologize. I really am happy for you. Besides, being on Sea Sprite has been quite therapeutic for me. I've realized a lot about my old life, including Aaron, and I'm better off here. Without him."

"And with me!" Twilight called from Shea's arms.

"Yes, Twi, with you."

The line moved forward as the enchanted kiosk accepted quite a few travelers for the next train to Meadowsweet, including a shifter still in his black bear form. I guess their

ID still worked while shifted. The other two lines got to go next, and then our turn came.

I inserted my ID into the kiosk, which magically scanned me to confirm my identity. With a little ding, I passed the test and gained admittance.

We all crossed under the arch to the train platform together. The mint car awaited us, and while it looked just like any other train car, it didn't sit on a pair of tracks like I'd expected. It must have moved via magic. We gathered on the concrete with the other patrons, Twilight squirming in Shea's arms, while Sunset slept in Zori's backpack.

When the doors opened, Zori went first, tripping over her own shoes, but she caught herself with a well-timed burst of air. My lips parted as I stepped inside after Shea. "Whoa." No plastic seats here. No scratched windows. No funky smells.

Rows of sea-blue velvet chairs lined both sides of the car. While the ceiling was white, dark wood paneling lined the walls. The same wood curved along the ceiling in thin strips at intervals marked by beautiful art deco light fixtures.

"You're blocking the door," Azura said, taking my shoulders from behind to steer me to two seats. "It's nothing like human transportation, right?"

"Maybe fancy European trains, but not American public transportation." I sat next to her, our hips brushing.

Twilight hopped over from Shea's seat to plaster herself against me. "So excited."

"Wait, Twi, how did you come to me on Sunday morning if not via a portal?"

She moved her shoulders in a little kitty shrug. "Familiar magic."

Okaaay.

Before the doors shut, a woman in a hot-pink wheelchair rolled on, and I watched as the train rearranged itself for her. Two of the seats disappeared. She wheeled into the spot and set her brakes, and the train released strands of magic to strap her down.

Then a bell sounded and the train lurched.

"YES!" Twilight shouted.

We couldn't see out the front or back of the train, but the side windows revealed a soft jade light growing as we moved forward. After a few seconds, it engulfed us but started to fade just as quickly.

The train eased to a stop. "That's it?" Twilight asked. I had to agree.

Azura's melodious laugh filled the space when she saw the look on my face. "It's quite short, but that's the point. Straight from one location to another."

"Good point."

We disembarked into a similar station. Twilight was still upset, so we tucked her into Zori's magically lightweight pack with Sunset, hoping the snuggles would cheer her up.

It did, but that meant she commented on everything we passed in Meadowsweet. "Oh, Kinley! Did you see the pizza place with the pink sign?" We'd been standing in front of it, so yes, I had. "Kinley! They have an escape room called Clue-less." I suppose we had to come back to Meadowsweet to do a mystery-themed escape room.

All three of my companions had visited Meadowsweet regularly, so they navigated the tree-filled Northern California town with ease—Shea in her raven form so she wouldn't have to walk on her pained joints. I could see the first traces of fall on the leaves above us, illuminated by the setting sun. The air felt a bit warmer here than on Sea Sprite, but still cool, so I tucked my hands in my jacket pockets.

After about ten minutes, we came upon Meadowsweet College. It looked like any other campus, with tall brick buildings broken up by courtyards and other gathering spaces. We cut through, passing groups of witches practicing spellwork and a very drunk fairy fraternity. Eventually, we came to an open field with bleachers on either side that Zori had recognized from @twistiewistie95's videos. Zori had flown here herself many times, so she knew just where to go.

"People use this place for frisbee golf, witchball, stuff like that," Zori said. She set her backpack down and let the familiars out.

I held my breath as I searched the field for our target. Lots of broom riders soared above us, but they moved so quickly that I couldn't identify them. It had seemed like Wisteria came here most nights, or at least posted a video from here wearing a different outfit, so I crossed my fingers she was up there.

Shea squawked at us and took off into the airborne crowd. "I'll help look," Zori said, pulling out her transparent broomstick and extending it to its full size. She tugged on her goggles and took off.

"I'll stay with you," Azura said. "I don't need to take a broom to the face today. Fairies fly slower than ravens and brooms."

"We can check the ground." I scanned the folks on the left side of the grass, not seeing a bleach-blond witch anywhere. "Did you get held up at work today?"

Azura's wings wiggled. "Yes, but in a good way! The Sea Sprites often congregate not far from our hotel, but they don't always travel down to our little stretch where the forest and beach become one. I think the musicians we hired for happy hour drew them in tonight, or maybe the sprites just felt like it, but they came through the trees and danced for us."

"We got to see them too!" Twilight said, jumping into my arms. "Tell her."

I explained the sprite's visit to my house during yoga.

"Kinley, what an honor. Your arrival on Sea Sprite must be truly bless—"

Sunset startled her as he took off past us, faster than I thought a red panda could run. We followed him to two women landing maybe thirty feet away. Shea joined us, shifting back.

"Oh, I'm so sorry. I didn't see you there." Zori turned and winked at us through her goggles.

The other woman pushed hers up so fast they caught in her platinum blond ponytail. "You almost knocked me out of the sky."

"But I caught you with my air magic." Zori gave her a full, winning smile. "Please, forgive me, Twistie Wistie."

Wisteria tossed her hair, seemingly pleased at being recognized. "Just don't let it happen again."

Before she could take off on her blue lightning-bolt broom, I ran up and pulled Zori to my side. "Oh my cauldrons, did you run into Twistie Wistie?" I looked at our suspect. "You're her, right?"

All her anger fell away now that she had admirers. "That's me!"

I held Twilight out. "My familiar and I are huge fans. She insists we watch your videos every night."

Wisteria waved a hand. "Oh, stop. You'll make me blush."

"Can we get your autograph?"

"Of course!" She pulled out a chunky pink pen. "Where should I sign?"

After tucking Twilight under one arm, I extracted a piece of paper from my tote. "Right here at the bottom."

She took it from me, and her smile died, replaced by thin, furious lips. "What's this?" she asked.

"You know what it is," I said. "A photocopy of a note you wrote threatening a woman who was recently murdered."

She snapped her gray eyes to mine, drinking in my features. "You're the one in all the Hijinx and CharmChat videos. The one everyone thinks killed Denise."

"Yes. But I'd just met her that day. You clearly had a bigger issue with Denise. What did she do to your sister?"

Wisteria crumpled up the copy and let it tumble from her fingers, but Zori caught it with her air magic, raising it back up to our suspect's eye level.

I sighed and pulled out my new phone. "Look, you either talk to us or I live stream on CharmChat that you threatened Denise. I bet if I put that letter online, someone will recognize your handwriting. Not only that, Denise recorded every transaction she made. We know you were one of her *special* customers."

She seethed. "I should have known Denise would continue to plague me even from beyond the grave." Wisteria held a hand up. "Oh, don't look at me like that. I didn't put her in the grave. I just broke her wrist."

My friends and I exchanged glances. Finally, the answer to the mystery of the broken wrist.

"How did you keep it from healing?" Shea asked.

Wisteria gave her a devilish grin. "I'm a healing witch, and the magic goes both ways. We can just as easily use our magic to harm the body as heal it. It's considered heinous to do so, but Denise deserved it."

Zori looked shocked and a little disgusted.

"Why?" I asked. "The letter says she cursed your sister, but we found you in Denise's ledger. You didn't hire her for that purpose?"

I could hear her teeth grinding from several feet away.

"We need to know everything, Wisteria," Azura said, her wings beating twice, "but we aren't detectives. We can't arrest you, and frankly, we don't care."

"Fine." Wisteria cracked her neck. "I hired Denise to create a cursed to-do list pad with tear-off sheets. With each list my sister would make, the curse would grow a little stronger. The curse was supposed to make her appear gradually more unstable. She loves lists, and uses them more in hard times, so I knew, the more unstable she got, the more she'd rely on making lists. I wanted...I wanted her boyfriend to break up with her because I was in love with him. When that happened, I'd destroy the pad, and the curse would lift."

"So what actually happened?" Zori asked, trying but failing to keep her tone neutral.

"Denise put the wrong curse on the pad. My sister ended up in the hospital dying after just a few uses. I put all my energy and magic into saving her." She stared Zori down. "Despite what you might think, I love my sister. I couldn't let Denise get away with her mistake."

Zori nodded. "I'm glad your sister is okay."

"How do we know you only broke Denise's wrist?" Shea asked. "You could have come back for more."

Wisteria rolled her eyes. "I got my revenge. Denise looked over her shoulder every day for months before I finally broke her wrist. The note and my little observation about her cookie-of-the-day habit scared her. I left her a few little gifts on her porch too, just to ratchet up the fear. The wrist was the culmination. Lots of people hated Denise, and I'm certainly not the only person to have threatened her."

"She said that like she knows that for sure," Twilight told me. I patted her head.

"That sounds like more than an assumption," I said.

Wisteria glared at us. "Why should I tell you anything else? You harassed and threatened me. Accused me of *murder*."

Shea threw an arm around my shoulder, pulling me against her. Zori did the same from the other side. Azura came up behind me and put her arms around all of us. Sunset crawled onto my head, his scarf hanging in my face. And Twilight tucked herself even closer to me.

Tears filled my eyes at their show of support.

"Because," Shea said. "People are accusing our girl here of murder too. We're sorry for being so aggressive with you, but put yourself in her shoes. If you know someone threatened Denise, please tell us."

"We'll keep you out of it," Azura assured her.

Wisteria looked amongst all of us, and finally, her shoulders fell. "Nice scarves," she told the familiars, who chittered happily. "I spied on Denise a lot as part of my plan. She had a lot of interesting interactions, but she had several with the same person. The last one got quite spicy when she slapped Denise and told her she'd 'get what's coming to her one of these days.'"

"Who was it? And when?" I asked, my heart rate accelerating faster than the brooms above.

"About three months ago. She's actually a pretty well-known fairy. Hang on." Wisteria pulled her phone out of her jacket. "Lots of people follow her on CharmChat."

My stomach sank, already knowing what I'd find when Wisteria showed us her screen.

Bethina Solanum, Sea Sprite's in-demand dentist.

Shea pulled away from our group hug, and the others split off too. Except Twilight, of course.

"Wait, you said *three* months ago?" Shea asked.

Wisteria nodded. "Yes, in June."

I sucked in a breath. "When Shea and I looked at Denise's smear campaign of Dr. Solanum's dental practice, the last post was from *six* months ago. Why would Dr. Solanum be arguing with and threatening Denise three months after that?" I pulled out my phone to double-check the hashtag Denise used. "Yes, Denise posted for four months, from November to March."

"Oh!" Twilight wormed around under my arm. "Black-mail. Maybe Dr. Solanum was paying Denise to stop her online bullying."

I snapped my fingers and swiped on my phone until I reached the photos of the blackmail ledger. "Wisteria, what's Dr. Solanum's username?"

She read it to me. "Dr. Solanum Knows Teeth."

"D-S-K-T! That's the other code in the blackmail ledger." I zoomed in. "But these payments go back before November. They started eighteen months ago in March of *last year*."

Azura frowned. "So the blackmail has nothing to do with the social media smear campaign?"

I pulled up the photos from the other secret ledger that logged all of Denise's nefarious customer transactions and looked for DSKT. Sure enough, I found an entry for a substantial amount of money from one month before the blackmail began.

"Dr. Solanum bought something illegal from Denise in February last year, and Denise turned around and black-mailed her a month later," I said. But Denise hadn't record-ed *what* Dr. Solanum had ordered. The column to notate if she'd bought poisoned stationery or one of the other usual items was blank.

"What?" Zori's eyes widened. "Dr. Solanum hired Denise? But she's so nice!"

Shea shook her head. "Nice people do bad things—and it must have been bad to get her blackmailed over it."

I sighed. "Would she kill to end the blackmail? That's the question."

"Only one person can answer that," Azura said.

"Twilight, I think my tooth hurts again."

Chapter Twenty-Two

"My face has frozen, Twilight. This island feels much colder than Portland." Especially before seven in the morning on a bicycle.

"Well, it's surrounded by the ocean, so *obviously*. You should have gotten a scarf to wrap around your face when you ride your bike! We could match. You could learn a charm to keep your cheeks warm too."

I eased the bike to a stop in front of the bike rack at Dr. Solanum's office. "What a wonderful idea. Magic still doesn't occur to me as a solution." I dismounted and snapped my bike lock into place. After removing my helmet and shaking out my raven hair, I picked Twilight up and tucked her into the front of my jacket for warmth.

"Now we wait."

Thirty seconds later, Twilight declared, "This is sooo boring."

We didn't have to wait long, thank frick, because she entertained herself by naming everything she could see. *Everything*.

As I'd expected, Dr. Solanum arrived to work bright and early. With jingling keys in hand and her loose silver curls bouncing, she approached the front doors of the clinic... and paused, brow furrowed, when she saw me. "Oh, hello. Is your tooth still bothering you?"

I took a quick look around to confirm no one else could hear us. A couple people approached on the sidewalk, a ghost floated not far behind them, and a bicycle turned into the next parking lot, but they were at a safe distance. "No. I've come to speak with you about Denise."

Dr. Solanum's wings beat twice. "Denise? What about her?"

"I know she was blackmailing you."

She lost the little color in her cheeks and her wings froze. The dentist stared for a long moment before rushing forward. She unlocked the door, grabbed my arm, and dragged me inside.

Twilight looked up from against my chest. "Want me to bite her?"

I shook my head.

Dr. Solanum dropped my arm once we got behind the front counter. "Come to my office." The smaller-than-expected room took up the back corner of the clinic. It felt as sterile as a patient room with its bare, bright-white furniture, like she'd used one of her teeth bleaching kits on her desk, cabinets, and chairs. Did she realize that the teeth-like furniture combined with the pink walls basically put us inside a mouth?

I dismissed my awkward thoughts, blaming it on the migraine brewing behind my eyes. The overhead fluorescents reflecting off the snowy furnishings made my head throb. After unzipping my jacket, I lifted Twilight out so her teeth and claws would be available should the doc decide to murder me.

Our suspect removed her blue jacket and sat in her white swivel chair that had cutouts to accommodate her wings. "I don't know what you're talking about. Denise must have been blackmailing someone else."

Twilight let out a mrow of disbelief.

"Nice try," I said, pushing my migraine glasses up my nose. "Denise kept a coded ledger that points to your social media account. Two people saw you arguing with her as well. One incident occurred only months ago, but Denise's ex-husband also saw you arguing before their separation. At first, I assumed your arguments had to do with Denise's online smear campaign against your business, but the dates don't match. I checked. Then I decoded your name in Denise's sales ledger."

Bethina blinked a few times. "You seem very well informed for a new witch in a new town."

"Denise rented her shop from me. I found her ledgers before the police warded the space. She covered her tracks well. But I'm a bibliowitch. I saw right through her invisible ink. Before you get any ideas, I'm not the only one who knows all this."

With a snort, she tucked her curls behind her pointed ears. "Don't worry, I'm not about to release one of my drills on you. I took an oath to heal, not harm." She ran both index fingers over her spotless desk. "You aren't going to leave until I tell you everything, are you?"

Twilight climbed onto her desk and stretched out.

"Looks like we're staying a while," I said.

Dr. Solanum nodded. "Denise helped me with something eighteen months ago."

I held a hand up. "You *hired* her," I corrected.

"Yes. I hired her." She bit her lip. "I ran for mayor last year. The campaign cost more than expected. I bled money."

Twilight gave me a questioning look. "Did she try to curse her competitor's stationery or something? Mayor Adel?"

"We don't understand," I told Bethina. "How could Denise help with your campaign? Didn't she trade in poison, curses, invisible ink?"

"She did. But I'd also heard that she had an affinity for making special pens."

Like those she made for Tyler and his cheating college customers. How could that help? Unless... "Did she make pens to influence what box someone checked on the ballot?"

"No. Bear with me. As I said, money grew tight. If I could know that I'd win the campaign, I'd have gladly kept spending. But only if I *knew*. I went to Madam Malfina. She couldn't help me—no visions came to her—and she's the best. So, I knew I needed more than regular seer magic."

Her cheeks went as pink as the walls. "Please know that I'm not proud of this. I consider it to be the worst thing I've ever done. I let the prospect of power influence me, and well...I went too far."

My brow pinched, and from the way Twilight's whiskers twitched, I could tell she felt just as confused. "Okay, we'll try to reserve judgment."

"Living on Sea Sprite, especially as a fairy, I was well aware that sea sprites are powerful seers, but they don't perform upon request."

I felt my stomach clench, and I had to clamp my fingernails into my palms to keep from launching across the desk.

Twilight had no such control. Her hackles rose, and she flung herself at Dr. Solanum. "Did you hurt a sea sprite? Or kill one? I'll tear your eyes out, lady!"

Dr. Solanum snapped her fingers and Twilight froze in mid-air. I stood, ready to do...something, but Bethina said to my familiar, "Just let me tell you the rest, okay?" She met my angry gaze. "You can grab her."

With Twilight in my arms, I sat back down. "Continue."

She took a deep breath. "I knew from a friend, who I absolutely will not name, that Denise had her side business and criminal contacts. I thought perhaps she could procure sea sprite dew, which you don't actually have to harm a sprite to get. At least, not really. You just trap them, take the dew from their wings, and release them."

"Right," I said, my voice hard. "I'm sure they undergo no psychological damage from that."

She gripped the edge of the desk. "I know, but at the time, I convinced myself only negligible damage would occur." After clearing her throat, she continued. "The dew can't be worked with in its raw form. Very few people know how to use it. I thought perhaps Denise could enchant it into one of her pens. Seers sometimes perform automatic writing, where their visions spill out of them via pen and paper. I thought it might be like that."

"So, Denise got the dew, turned it into an ink, and stuck it in a pen?"

"Yes. The ink was rather oily and hard to read, but it worked. I asked my question, got my answer, and pulled out of the election the same day. And immediately hated myself for what I'd done."

Oily ink. I straightened. "Was the ink black?"

"That's correct."

Denise had ten bottles of black, oily ink in her secret room. "Did you only indicate that you wanted the one pen?"

She lifted an eyebrow. "Yes."

"Given what you paid her, I'm assuming the dew didn't run cheap."

"No, Denise paid a lot for the dew, so she charged me a lot. I used the entire pen for one question. The magic ate through all the ink inside it."

Why would Denise have so many extra bottles of ink if the dew cost so much? Had she continued to sell these premonition pens? None of the codes in her ledger seemed to indicate she had. Unless we were wrong about what the codes meant.

"Ask her about the blackmail," Twilight said.

Right. "How long after did Denise first blackmail you?"

"Weeks. That's when her husband saw us arguing. I made for an easy target. She knew I had a lot to lose with my business, especially with my social media presence. She also knew how sacred sea sprites are to fairies, so my crime went beyond unforgivable. And she knew I could make regular payments."

"Did you even save money? If you had kept going in your campaign, would you have spent more than you paid Denise?"

She sighed. "The blackmail would have cost more. I tried underpaying her. That's when she started the smear campaign. When we argued a few months ago, I was trying to get her to lower the payments. But she was ruthless. I would have spent way more on the blackmail than the campaign over the years to come, but Denise's death freed me from that. I know that doesn't look good for me." She looked at her palms. "But I have enough dew on my hands already. I didn't need to add blood too."

I wasn't sure if the tears gathering beneath her lashes or the droop to her wings convinced me, but I believed her. My eyes dropped to Twilight, who nodded.

But if not Dr. Solanum, then who killed Denise? My gut told me it had something to do with what we'd just learned. The sea sprite ink felt like the missing piece, but I didn't understand how.

Twilight and I left Dr. Solanum to sit in silence, still staring at her hands. Neither of us spoke as we prepared to ride away. I was so lost in thought that I almost didn't see a jogger in orange shorts, just like Zori's crush, Georgina, had worn at Mystic Mugs the day before.

I hit the brakes and Twilight jolted in the basket.

"Kinley! Are you okay? What happened?"

"Foxglove Point!" I yelled, a touch too loudly. A few pedestrians gave me curious looks.

Georgina had seen Denise arguing with two men at Foxglove Point two months ago. Azura had told me the sea sprites frequented the area near her family's hotel. Another time, she'd mentioned the hotel was near Foxglove Point. Could the men have been poachers?

Any interference with the sea sprites, including trapping them and assaulting them for their dew, would surely be punished harshly. The magical legal system remained a mystery to me, but such a crime must equal a severe felony. Only dangerous people would go into sea sprite poaching, and considering Denise argued with the two men, it seemed she'd gotten on their bad side—as she tended to do.

I considered why the men might have been upset with her. Maybe Denise had only recently decided to start selling the premonition pens, but no one had bought one yet. Could she have taken the dew from the men on loan? Perhaps she still owed those men money for the dew, but without sales, couldn't pay them back. That could be a motive.

Or maybe that had nothing to do with it. Perhaps she'd tried to blackmail the poachers, threatened to turn them into the MBI. Could her minor blackmail success have made her think she could take on bigger fish?

Chapter Twenty-Three

"I still don't see the point of this." The man who smelled strongly of beer adjusted his jean shorts. "Just grab a book and let's go."

"Earl, you know I've wanted to come to Sea Sprite for ages just so I could come to The Perfect Page! I want the perfect book for me." Earl's wife pointed to her chest. "Not some random book." She kept approaching the sales counter, her sneakers squeaking on the wood floors.

He rolled his glassy eyes. "I still say all books are a waste of money. What's the point when you've got TV for free?"

"Yeah, like you ever let me decide what to watch," she muttered.

Twilight pushed to her feet on the counter. "This guy sounds like the worst."

I agreed. The shop would close in a few minutes, and this guy just had to be the last customer of the day.

Managing to pull her lips into a smile, the woman said, "Hello! I'd like to find the perfect book."

Page lit up the golden circles on the counter.

I smiled back, determined to give her an enjoyable experience. "Step right up! We always know just what your soul needs. Place your hands in the circles."

Earl huffed. "Maybe you'll get a book on weight loss. Your soul seems pretty desperate for it, considering how much of my money you spend on potions and exercise equipment."

Twilight's hackles rose, and so did mine.

Page, I might have to change the sign outside that says I'm not a criminal, because I think I'm about to become one. This guy is asking for a slap.

Yes, but have patience, Kinley. Trust me.

I forced a breath in and ignored the man, just as his wife had. She put her hands in the circles and light spread across them. Moments later, a book appeared in front of her.

How to Lose Your Husband in Ten Days: A Guide to a Quick Divorce by W.I. Stocks.

Twilight rolled onto her back and kicked her feet, laughing so hard I thought a furball would come up. I bit my cheeks to avoid doing the same.

Earl's cheeks, however, turned bright red as he faced me. "Is this a joke? What kind of operation are you running here?"

His soon-to-be ex-wife, I hoped, stared at the book for several long moments before she snatched it from the air. She reached into her purse, extracted a twenty-dollar bill, set it on the counter, and said, "Thank you so much. I can't tell you how much I need this book."

With that, she spun around. "You know, Earl, it seems I'm about to lose one-hundred-eighty pounds *very* quickly." Then she stormed out of the shop, Earl on her heels, pleading with her to stop.

"Ugh. *Earl* made me want to *hurl*," Twilight said when the door clicked closed.

That, of course, was the moment something sharp hurled through the front window, missing my head by two inches.

I clutched my chest and jolted to the side, my heart banging against my ribs. "What was that?"

A projectile. It landed in the wall behind you, Page said. His rich pulse of a voice, normally so unflappable in my mind, for once sounded quite *flapped*. Literally. A thousand pages flapped across my eardrums as everything in the store shivered with his anger.

"Holy hexes, a projectile!" Twilight said. "Did it touch you at all, Kinley?" She jumped off the counter. I assured her it hadn't grazed me, and we ran to the wall.

A four-inch obsidian arrowhead had penetrated the wall. The tip was buried, but cut into the wide end were the words "I TOLD YOU TO STOP."

Twilight hopped onto my shoulder to read the ominous carving. "The murderer," she whispered.

Around us, the shivering turned to jerking, wrenching, and falling as Page's fury made tables wobble, floorboards loosen, and books tumble.

How dare someone threaten my bonded witch!

The words quaked down my spine, but instead of stirring up my already inflamed emotions, they somehow calmed me. I rubbed the wall.

"Let Page be pissed," Twilight said. "I am too. Together, we'll crush the murderer beneath a pile of books while scratching out their—"

"Okay, you two," I said. "I appreciate your support. I do. But if we get upset, we're giving the killer what they want."

Page's seismic activity dwindled, but I could still feel his turmoil. With what felt like a pained sigh, he restored the bookshop to its orderly appearance, everything moving right back into place.

The door opened, and I turned to tell the newcomer that we were closed, but through the displays, I spotted Sylvie, with Dusk wrapped around her neck.

"Hello!" She waved. "We're here to show off Dusk's new scarf! It has little potion bottles on it."

Dusk waved around the ends of the purple scarf with his little raccoon hands.

"Very cute, Dusk. You look amazing," I said, trying to show enthusiasm despite the rather violent threat sticking out of the wall.

"Cool!" Twilight said. "Purple looks good with your gray fur."

He wagged his tail, but Sylvie stopped, tilting her head. "What's wrong?" Her eyes landed on the obsidian. "What is that?" She rushed forward to inspect the arrowhead. "Another threat. Well, what are you waiting for?" she asked, hands on her hips. "You promised."

I pulled out my phone. "I know."

Less than a minute later, Ryland stepped through a portal into the shop. He took one look at the arrow and a vein in his forehead pulsed.

Midnight popped out of Ryland's jacket pocket and flew around my head to inspect me, a stream of smoke pouring from his nostrils.

Ryland similarly cast his eyes over my face, my torso, my legs. "You're okay?"

I nodded. "It didn't touch me, but it came close. Too close."

Midnight settled on my free shoulder, meeped, and rubbed his face against mine. I reached up to stroke his tail. It was nice having Twilight on one shoulder and Midnight on the other.

"This just happened?" Ryland asked.

"Yes," I confirmed. "Minutes ago."

"Do you know why they threatened you?" He ruffled his blond locks. "And what they want you to stop doing?"

Tell him everything, Kinley, Page said. *The time has come.*

I ran my teeth over my lip. "Yes. This is actually the second warning they've sent."

Ryland stepped back. Running a hand along his jaw, he said, "Someone threatened you before, and you didn't tell me?" He flicked his eyes to Sylvie. "Did you know?"

Sylvie started to confess, but I held my hand up. "It's my fault. When the rock came through my living room window, I begged her not to tell you. I didn't want to stop investigating. If the killer had resorted to scaring me, I figured I knew something important. Maybe something you didn't."

Something akin to betrayal flashed in his eyes. "But if you'd just told me everything you knew, then I would have been working with all the information."

I tugged on the sleeves of my sweater. "I had my reasons not to tell you, but I'll tell you now. Minus a few minor details."

He put a gentle hand on my elbow and I stopped fussing with my sleeves. "Kin—"

"I won't leave out anything relevant, I promise."

Ryland released my arm. "Okay, I trust you." Midnight chirped his agreement.

Their confidence sent a pang of guilt through my chest. "Well, it started with the key I have to Denise's shop..."

Thirty minutes later, I'd told him everything, except I'd made it sound like I'd investigated with only Twilight's help. I'd also skipped over Tyler's name, leaving him out of it as we'd promised.

Ryland listened, and other than saying goodbye to Sylvie when she'd needed to get to an appointment, he didn't say a word. Just listened. After the first few minutes, we'd sat in one of the reading nooks. The familiars still perched on my shoulders, which had helped keep me talking through Ryland's silence.

"So, I think it might have something to do with the sea sprites and those guys Denise argued with. They could have been poachers she owed money to or otherwise upset."

He crossed his legs at the ankles, his grass-green sneakers complementing the darker rug. "I'm going to ignore the fact that you somehow broke through the ward on Denise's house, which clearly required an accomplice you won't name, and hid evidence from me. I know you want to clear your name. But, Kinley, I'm good at my job. I needed to find someone to reveal Denise's invisible ink. That took time, given the strength of her enchantment. It's amazing you saw right through it. Once we could read the ink, I realized she had an illegal second business. We performed an additional search of her house with more resources. We found the secret room. If you'd given me time, I'd have gotten to where you are now...without you getting death threats. You also could have shared information with me too, but I understand why you didn't think you could tell me." He tapped his knees. "Anyway, those two guys out at Foxglove Point? We caught them there a month ago. They were poaching, and they're locked up now. They couldn't have killed Denise."

My head fell back, almost dislodging the dragon and cat attached to me. I let out a frustrated sigh. "Maybe she knew other poachers."

"Maybe, but right now, all we can do is move on with the evidence we have." Pulling out his phone, he said, "You have the rock that came through your window in your closet?"

"Yes."

"Then that's our next stop. A geowitch will meet us at your house in a few minutes." Midnight started chittering. "Let's grab the arrowhead and portal over."

Twilight noticed the blank look on my face. "A geology witch. One whose primary magic focuses on rocks. They're fairly rare."

Midnight flew over to Ryland's shoulder and bounced up and down. "You excited to see Uncle Owen, buddy?"

"Uncle?" Twilight said. "Oh my god, we're about to meet the fam."

"Wow!" Owen, Ryland's brother, spun in a circle, seeming to absorb every detail of my living room. "Did you know sunflowers symbolize loyalty? I wonder if your grandmother valued loyalty." His gaze snagged on a bookshelf and he hurried toward it, bending over to read a little sign with a broomstick on it. "'Frequent Flyer.' That's hilarious!"

My eyes bounced between him and the owl circling the room, pausing occasionally to dive bomb Ryland and hoot at Midnight. The witch and his familiar made quite an energetic pair. They'd entered my house not two minutes ago and had instantly made themselves at home.

Ryland clapped an affectionate hand on his brother's flannel-clad back. "Owen, you haven't even met Kinley and Twilight yet."

Owen, who was even taller and broader than Ryland, turned from the bookshelf and flashed me a huge smile. "Sorry! This house is just so interesting."

I smiled back, feeling immediately charmed by this man. "Don't worry. My first time here, the house captivated me too. You should see the upstairs bathroom. And meet Mark."

Mischief gleamed in his eyes. "I would *love* to meet Mark, whoever that is, and please, please show me the bathroom."

"Oh, I like him," Twilight said from her spot on the back of the couch.

I laughed, ready to take him straight to the bathroom, but Ryland said, "How about after you look at the rock and arrowhead?"

"Okay, Mr. Detective." Owen winked at me and wove through the furniture to where I stood at the room's entrance. He grabbed my hand and shook. "I'm Owen, but I'm sure you knew that. You're Kinley, but I'm sure you knew that too." He pointed to his owl. "That's N-o-o-t, Noot, spelled thusly because it rhymes with hoot." On cue,

Noot hooted. "And before you ask, yes, the kids used to call me Owlen after Noot became my familiar."

"Oh, I *really* like him," Twilight said. Of course she did. Owen was as excited about everything as she was.

He kept shaking my hand while I chuckled. "Nice to meet you, Owlen. And you too, Noot. It's a good thing you're an owl and not a rabbit." I flashed Ryland a mischievous smile.

Midnight let out a series of snorts, and Owen grabbed onto Ryland. "Cursed cauldrons, I knew I liked her. In town for less than a week and she knows about your deep terror of all things rabbit related?"

Ryland shook his brother off. "Page told her. Kinley, you and Page will be a dangerous combination. So much gossip."

"Don't forget Twilight." I gestured to my familiar. "Owen, that's Twilight, and she really likes you."

He bowed to her. "I love your scarf. It's quite fetching."

The cat walked the back of the couch like a real catwalk.

Ryland came to my side. "Twilight started a trend. I need to stop at The Witch Stitch. Midnight wants a scarf."

"She's a fashionista," I said.

"Speaking of fashion," Owen said. "I hear my brother found you so irresistible in your wedding dress that he stole you away to Sea Sprite."

Ryland's ears twitched and turned slightly pink. "Very funny."

Owen bumped his shoulder into Ryland's. "Did you seriously have to resort to tackling a bride in order to get one close to—"

A portal opened behind Owen, and Ryland tackled him through it, leaving me and the three familiars in the living room. Noot and Midnight didn't seem surprised, which suggested this to be a common occurrence with the brothers. Moments later, another portal opened, and the brothers stepped through, both laughing.

"Okay, Kinley," Owen said. "I've been instructed to behave. So, please, show me your geological specimens."

Ryland and I had set both items in the kitchen, so with much enthusiasm, Owen got to meet Mark the sunflower in the hallway atrium on the way to the back of the house.

"Did you know I'm a kitchen witch?" Owen said after only a brief look around the kitchen. The restraint pained him. He absolutely wanted to open every drawer and cabinet. "Ryland is too."

"Not as good as you." Ryland squeezed his brother's shoulder. "He's the head chef at The Unicorn's Uncle. People come from all over to eat there."

"You're good enough to cook there too, but you're too busy with your silly portal and ward magic," Owen said, grabbing Ryland to give him the most warm-hearted noogie I'd ever seen. These two were *adorable*.

"Oooh, ask him if they have fish!" Twilight said.

"Twilight wants to know if you have fish. I want to know why it's called The Unicorn's Uncle."

Owen gave me a thoroughly confused look. "Why not?" He nodded to Twilight. "And you can have all the fish you want." He rubbed his hands together before throwing his arms wide. "Now, I'll need complete silence."

Ryland rolled his eyes. We came to stand next to each other on one side of the kitchen island, while Owen stood on the other, the rocks between us.

After smoothing his hands over both rocks, Owen started with the one that crashed into my window. He rested his hands on it and closed his eyes. After a few seconds, a line formed between his brows. We all watched intently, the only sound the soft swishing of Twilight's tail across the counter.

Five minutes passed before Owen opened his eyes. He said nothing, only moved on to the arrowhead. Wrapping it in his large hands, he shut his eyes again. After eight minutes, I began to fidget, my shoulder brushing Ryland's.

He gave me a reassuring smile, and I stilled.

Finally, with a sigh, Owen opened his eyes and set down the arrowhead.

Ryland put his hands on the counter. "Did you learn anything?"

"I tried to get *concrete* details, pun very much intended, but whoever worked with these rocks had so much emotion roiling through them that it clouded my vision. I could only get that they are very angry and bitter about something that they lost. Something magical."

I pushed away the disappointment that tried to lodge in my stomach. Owen may not have gotten specifics, but this could still be useful information. "Ry, could it be about the sea sprites? They're magical."

Owen smirked at my use of his brother's shortened name.

"Maybe," Ryland said. "But it could be about anything. Our entire world is magical. Owen, did you get any sense of what the person looked like? Or anything else?"

He shook his head. "No, sorry. I'm sure they used rocks to threaten Kinley instead of paper so she couldn't use her bibliomancy on the threats, but that's more of a logical deduction than anything the rocks told me."

"Agreed," Ryland said. "I appreciate your help."

We saw Owen out. He lived only a few minutes away, so he didn't bother with a portal.

When the door shut, Ryland turned to me. "Our people are working on decoding Denise's customers. I emailed that the codes refer to social media handles, or at least some of them do. That should help them identify more of her customers. It's possible one of them killed her, or it's possible one of the customers' *targets* did."

"Like if Denise cursed a piece of stationery, the victim of that curse tracked her down and killed her?"

"Exactly."

My stomach sank. "It will take so long to track down all her customers and their victims."

His eyes twinkled. "Yes, but in the meantime, I have another idea. You said Page taught you to read ink and paper?"

"Yes, why?"

"Good, stay here. I'm going to break into the evidence locker."

Chapter Twenty-Four

Breaking into the evidence locker apparently consisted of simply portaling in and out in about thirty seconds. Which I appreciated, because my heart had jumped into my throat the moment Ryland disappeared.

He'd reappeared with a bottle of the oily, black ink that Shea had said smelled of the ocean, which I now knew contained sea sprite dew.

"No one can ever know about this, Kin." Ryland slid the ink into my hand. "We put everything from Denise's secret room into evidence, and I could lose my job for taking this without authorization. But if you can learn something from the ink, it's worth it."

Midnight meeped his agreement from Ryland's shoulder.

I rolled the bottle between my fingers. "Back at Denise's, I already tried. Nothing happened when I held it, even though I could easily tell the other bottles held invisible ink and compulsion ink."

Ryland's face fell, but Twilight put a paw on my leg. "You told me how scared you were to use your magic that night. You thought you might blow up the little room with your friends inside it. Didn't you hold back? Not only that, but Page taught you to go deeper with your magic."

I squatted down to pat her head. "You're a smart one, you know that?"

"Of course, I do."

Chuckling, I stood back up. "Twilight reminded me that I held back that night, and that I didn't know what I was doing then. I should try again. C'mon." We still stood in the foyer, so I grabbed Ryland's sleeve and tugged him back to the living room.

We sat on the couch, our knees touching. Twilight curled up on my other side. I pulled a long breath in through my nose. "Okay, here goes noth—well, I hope something."

Holding back would get me nowhere, so I reached straight for my warm pond of baby-pink magic and dove in headfirst. Magic spread across my limbs, into my bones. I pushed it through my fingers and into the ink vial. It heated, almost searing my skin, but I held on.

A strong sense of peace hit me first, followed by sorrow and terror and grief.

The sea sprites. I could feel their emotions, their usual state of tranquility followed by their anguish at having their dew stolen. I forced that to the side, searching for more.

New feelings hit me, this time bitterness. Resentment. Anger. I recognized the form of this temperament—Denise. She did not want to make this ink. But I couldn't see why. So, I pushed her emotions away too.

With that cleared, I could see the ink's physical properties. The oily dew. A couple typical ink ingredients—a resin and a dispersing agent—that my magic innately recognized. A spell to preserve the dew and keep the ingredients bound together. And something else...some ingredient unfamiliar to me.

I held the ingredient up with my magic, tasting it. Letting it sit on my mind's tongue, surprised to find it fresh, like pure rain with a dash of new soil. It tasted of renewal.

Whatever this was, Denise had added it to restore something, but in a way that somehow enhanced the dew.

Despite trying, I couldn't determine how it enhanced the dew, or pull anything else from the ink, so I slowly released my magic and opened my eyes.

Twilight perched on the edge of the coffee table with her pupils wide and her whiskers twitching. Ryland had his phone in hand with Sylvie's contact info pulled up. Midnight held his tail in his foreclaws.

They released a collective breath and started talking at the same time. Well, Midnight chirped.

"Kinley, wands and willows, you scared the fur out of me!" Twilight said, her tail smacking the table.

"Hexes, I thought you'd never come back!" Ryland slapped a hand to his heart. "I was about to call Sylvie to see if she knew what to do. She must have seen your grandmother use her magic loads of times."

I set the ink down next to Twilight and held my hands out, palms up. "I'm fine. Why did you get so worried? That only took a few minutes."

The three of them exchanged glances.

"That took forty minutes," Ryland said. "And you started crying at one point."

"Oh." Dried tears met my fingers when I brushed them across my cheeks. "I could feel the sea sprites' pain."

Speaking of pain, a thunderclap of electricity behind my eyes had me clutching my head and curling into myself.

"See, you are *not* fine!" Twilight said.

Ryland put a warm hand on my back, and that feeling of a towel straight from the dryer spread across my skin again. Was he using his magic intentionally? "Are you okay?"

"Migraine," I bit out. After a few labored breaths, the pain passed. I straightened. "That wasn't so bad. Maybe I just overdid it a bit with my magic."

"Do you need a potion?" he asked.

I shook my head. "No. I'm okay for now. I don't want to waste one if that was the worst of it. Let me tell you what I saw." I explained everything. "It's weird, right? Why add a restorative ingredient to the ink? And how would that enhance it?"

"I want to know why Denise felt so resentful about making the ink if someone paid her to do it," Ryland said.

"Maybe she just didn't like the customer," I said.

Twilight tilted her head. "Excellent point. She did hate a lot of people."

"Midnight says—" But before Ryland could tell me what Midnight said, his phone rang. "My boss." He swiped to answer. His boss started talking before Ryland could say anything. "Okay, I'll be right there."

Ryland twisted farther toward me on the couch, his lips pinched with worry. "I'm sorry, Kinley. There's an emergency on the other side of the island. An accident during a nature walk by the hotel. Some tourists were injured. I need to go portal them to the medical center."

"Oh no, that's awful. Go!"

He grabbed the ink, opened a portal, and hopped through with Midnight still on his shoulder.

"At least he said tourists, so you know Azura is safe."

I took my phone out of my back pocket to text her, anyway. She responded instantly that she was fine, but a rock slide hit three tourists before magic could stop it.

"Azura says she thinks the healers will easily fix them. That's good."

"Whew." Twilight sprawled on the coffee table, her long limbs stretched to one side. She let her head fall to the wood. "I'm sorry you had to feel the sea sprite's emotions."

I swallowed. "Yeah, I didn't enjoy that. But it was the only part of the ink that made sense to me. Why did Denise resent the ink so much? Why add the restorative ingredient? It feels important."

"Okay, let's focus on that," Twilight said. "Sea sprite dew provides visions of the future. It's powerful, right? Why would it need to be restored?" Her tail curled into a skeptical question mark.

"It wouldn't." I tucked my legs beneath me. "Maybe the ink was being used to restore something else."

Twilight flipped to her feet in one smooth motion. "Hang on. Owen told us the killer lost something magical."

"You're right! Let's assume the killer used the ink to restore something lost and magical." I gasped. "Twi, what if they lost *their* magic?"

"Only one type of witch would benefit from sea sprite dew to restore their magic."

I exhaled. "A seer." With a gurgled laugh, I said, "And who happened to live next door to Denise?"

Twilight's eyes widened. "Madam Malfina. That doesn't mean it's her, though. There are other seers on the island and plenty of others who could portal here."

"True." I closed my eyes and let everything I knew about the seer ascend. "Zori said Martha stopped doing predictions for a while after her son died. Could she have completely lost her ability to see because of grief?"

I opened my eyes to see Twilight pacing the little table. "It's possible. Didn't Zori also say Malfina does her predictions behind the scenes now, instead of in front of her customers? Maybe she uses the pens to do predictions in private so no one knows her magic is gone."

"Yes. Wouldn't she go through a lot of pens that way, though? Dr. Solanum needed a whole pen for one question. Even if she's doing fewer predictions these days, that would add up fast." I snapped my fingers. "Unless the restorative property of the ink allows *her* magic to work."

Twilight paused. "You mean when Martha uses the pen, the sea sprite dew combines with her seer magic to provide a prediction, and that requires less ink than only the sea sprite dew?"

I shrugged. "Maybe. This is all speculation." After grabbing my phone again, I opened CharmChat. "Let's try to get some proof." Finding Madam Malfina's profile took only seconds: @madam_malfina_sees. I pulled up the photos of Denise's ledger on my phone and searched her transactions for a customer coded as MMS.

"Nothing. Madam Malfina isn't here."

Twilight's furry brow furrowed. "Why wouldn't Denise record the transactions?"

I chewed on my lip. "Maybe we're wrong. Or maybe Denise didn't use Malfina's social media as her code. Let's try something else."

I texted Zori to ask if she knew when Madam Malfina started doing predictions again. "Maybe we can compare the approximate date she resumed seeing to when Denise first made the premonition pens."

My phone buzzed.

Zori: It was sometime after the Lights of Love festival in February last year. I remember because she always has a popular booth there, but she missed last year. I don't think it was long after, though.

My spine straightened. "The Lights of Love festival. Tabitha mentioned it at the bakery."

"You're right!" Twilight bounced on her toes. "Tabitha said she almost looked inside Denise's nightly trash deposit in the bakery dumpster the night of the festival, but she didn't because Madam Malfina was watching her!"

"What if Madam Malfina looked in the trash? Maybe she heard Tabitha ask Denise why she always threw her trash away there, and Malfina wanted to see for herself. The festival was in February, so that was around the time Denise made the pen for Dr. Solanum."

I opened up my witchernet browser and searched for when Dr. Solanum pulled out of the mayoral race, which would also tell us when Denise made the first premonition pen. Then I looked up the festival date to compare. "Twilight, she ended her bid for mayor the day after the festival. Dr. Solanum told us she nixed the campaign the same day she got the pen from Denise. So, Denise must have made the pen the night before."

"Which means Denise made the pen the night of the festival, and if Malfina went through her trash that same night, maybe she recognized the sea sprite dew on scraps of garbage. She knew Denise could use the dew."

Twilight and I locked eyes as something clicked. "What if Madam Malfina wasn't a *customer* at all? Maybe she collected evidence against Denise and blackmailed *her* into making the ink. Denise would have needed a lot of money to buy all the dew..."

"Which is why Denise started blackmailing Dr. Solanum and Tyler only a few weeks later." Twilight's ears went flat. "This all comes back to Madam Malfina."

A dull thumping from the hallway told me Mark had started tapping on the atrium glass, as if he could sense our excitement at sliding all the pages of this murder manuscript into place.

Twilight resumed pacing, her scarf bouncing at her neck. "Malfina got everything she wanted. So why kill Denise?"

I flopped back on the couch as my enthusiasm deflated. "Right, we need motive. Maybe Denise got tired of it and threatened to tell everyone that Malfina couldn't see anymore without the pens? But then Malfina could send Denise to prison for her criminal activities."

"Mutually assured destruction."

"Exactly." Little black spots with yellow halos flashed in my eyes. I reached beneath my glasses to rub along my eyelids. There went my hopes that a full migraine wouldn't come. Some people got hours after visual disturbances before the pain hit. Not me. I likely had minutes, so I kept pushing my thoughts forward. "Denise would have wanted out of her situation. She would've tried to gain leverage. Denise's ex said she watched the neighborhood constantly.

Maybe she turned all that attention on Malfina and learned something that would turn the tables."

Mark's tapping grew faster.

"Mark, we hear you!" Twilight called.

My familiar reached one end of the coffee table, turned around, and walked toward the other. "What would be enough to turn the tables? Unless...if Malfina killed Denise, maybe she killed someone before?"

"Twi..." I let my hand fall as something clicked about the only other death in Malfina's life that I knew about. "When you told me about primary and secondary magic, you said that some families think having more than one primary magic waters down their hereditary specialty. Did you say seer families think like that?"

"Yes, they do," a hard-as-stone voice said.

Twilight and I whipped our heads to the hallway to find a short woman in a red fleece jacket pointing a golden wand at us, two bolts of magic hovering at its tip.

Chapter Twenty-Five

"You should have listened to your sunflower," Malfina said, taking a few steps into the living room. Gone was the kind woman who'd reassured me when we'd first met. In her place stood someone ruthless and severe. "You should have spelled your back door too."

I'd locked the door, but spelled it? Maybe I should have learned that instead of how to clean a coin.

"Now, put your hands up," she said.

My eyes locked onto the yellow bolts at her wand tip, and as much as my muscles wanted to freeze, I forced my arms to lift.

Malfina waved her wand, and a small clump of gray hair slipped from her bun. "Ligare!" The two bolts shot at us, and my chest constricted, but the neon magic ensnared my hands, binding my wrists way too tight. Poor Twilight ended up with all four paws tied together. Her distressed mewling broke my heart.

"I'd tell you to shut your familiar up, but I put a spell on the house. No one can hear anything going on inside these walls."

"Let her go," I seethed. "You want me, not her. No one else can hear her talk, anyway."

The seer's lip curled. "Right, I'm sure she won't tell your MBI friend's little dragon familiar everything."

Twilight shot me an offended look. "I wouldn't leave you here, anyway, Kinley!"

"I did warn you days ago," Malfina said, stepping up to the couch with her wand pointed at my heart. "This morning, outside the dental clinic, I heard you yelling about Foxglove Point. So I warned you *again*. Did you think I'd stop watching after the arrowhead? I don't leave things to chance. I follow through."

Of course, she'd spied on me. I'd even seen her outside The Witch Stitch on Tuesday and inside Mystic Mugs yesterday. This was all my fault. Less than one week on Sea Sprite and I'd mortally endangered my new familiar and myself. I'd finally found a place I felt like I could just be *Kinley*, and I was about to lose it. How could I lose two lives in two locations in one week?

Our only chance was for Ryland to come back. If he portaled the injured tourists quickly, maybe he'd return in time to help. But I had a wand trained on me. I had to distract her, keep her talking. "A seer who doesn't leave things to chance, huh? You prefer to see the outcome, I suppose?"

"Of course. The things I see always come to pass. Always."

"If you're so good, why didn't you anticipate *losing* your magic? Or did you see it? Did you know you'd lose it but decided it was worth it?"

Twilight side-eyed me. "Are you trying to enrage our captor?"

Lights flashed across my eyes in diagonal lines, reminding me a migraine fast approached. I should have taken that potion. Could the migraine have worse timing?

Malfina's nostrils flared, and another wisp of hair shook free from her bun. "Of course not! Seers can't know everything. You think if I'd known I'd lose my magic that I'd have—" She stopped talking, her lips sealing into a tight line.

"That you'd have killed your son? Don't worry, I already figured that out."

"*What!?*" Twilight wriggled on her back, looking between me and Malfina.

"She's a geowitch," I explained. "Her son died in a tragic accident. A section of cliffs along the beach fell on him, remember? We found out at The Witch Stitch. And what happened tonight? Some rocks came down on tourists near the hotel, calling Ryland away from us just before Malfina got here."

"Heckin' hexes, this is bad, Kinley." Twilight turned pleading eyes on me. "You need to do something. Have another magical explosion! Like you did in Portland!"

How did I make that happen? I tried to dial up my panic, but my heart was already about to shoot through my ribs. I reached for my magic, trying to thrust it through my skin.

C'mon. Explode out of me! Destroy the house for all I care. Just don't hurt Twilight!

Then I remembered Page promising me that, as long as I stayed bonded to him, his magic would calm mine. Even if I freaked out, a repeat of my bridal suite wouldn't happen.

Wonderful. Just wonderful.

Malfina, oblivious to all of this, jabbed her wand forward. "I knew you'd worked out that I was a geowitch, since you asked about seer families shunning additional primary magics. I didn't know how far you'd thought things through, though. Excellent job. I did kill my son. And when I saw you bring in the detective's brother—I'd forgotten about him, a rookie mistake—I knew I needed to separate you and the detective. I flew over and dropped the rocks on the tourists, then flew back. Here's a gold star." She traced the wand in front of me until a shining star formed. It shot forward and burst into an array of light right in front of my face.

A battalion of pain signals stabbed, shot, and blasted through my eyes, forehead, and jaw as my migraine finally arrived.

"Kinley!" Twilight yelled.

Malfina laughed. "I didn't expect that. How fun. I wish I could have done that to Denise."

I choked back my nausea and, as well as I could, thrust my restrained hands out to steady myself on the couch. "She figured out you killed him too, didn't she? Denise would have watched you, looking for anything to use against you. You must have slipped up. Done something to reveal yourself as a geowitch. She lived next to you, after all. Just one look through a window..."

Malfina's wand shook as the lines on her face tightened with fury. "Denise was always a nosy little worm. She couldn't just keep to herself and make my pens!"

Twilight rolled her eyes as she twisted around on the coffee table, clearly hoping somehow to slip her magical restraints. "Malfina could have just not killed her son."

"After she worked out that you killed him, I assume she refused to keep supplying you with the pens. You both had criminal leverage over each other at that point. Why not just start buying the pens from her?"

She scoffed. "You think I have that kind of money? She told me I'd have to pay her back for all the money she spent on the ink, plus interest, first." Interesting, considering Denise had blackmailed that money from others. "I don't have that kind of money. Not after spending decades supporting a no-good, talentless son who bled me dry."

I almost asked why she didn't just cut him off, but then it clicked. "He had to have known about your geologic magic if he grew up in your house. Did he threaten to tell your entire family if you didn't support him all these years? Did you finally snap and kill him? I don't understand why your family knowing is such a big deal. Who cares?"

"That's easy for you to say! You know nothing of our world. You didn't spend your whole life hearing that seer magic is a divine gift that we should revere. That it can be eroded or taken away if the holder doesn't follow a specific way of life. That a second or, the moon forbid, a third primary magic indicates the seer is weak. Corrupted. *Impure.* You didn't watch your cousin kicked off the island when her fire magic burst from her hands one day. Or a friend in another town shunned by everyone she knew."

"Ragwort and rose," Twilight whispered. "Seers sound like some kind of cult."

I agreed, but something else stood out to me, and it gave me a tiny glimmer of hope. I thrust my pain aside and forced my thoughts to focus. "That all sounds absurd, and I'm sorry you've had to live with that judgment, but...you said they think seer magic could be taken away if you don't follow a specific way of life. Sounds like that part might have proved true considering you lost your magic after, you know, *murdering* your son. Your magic must not have totally left, though, if the premonition pens helped restore it during the few moments you used them. But now you've murdered Denise. Do you really want to make it worse by killing me and Twilight? You might never find a way to access even a sliver of your seer magic ever again if your body count keeps increasing."

"Oh, Kinley. I had to accept that I'd never access my magic again when I killed Denise. Nice try, though." She shook her head. "I'm more worried about covering my tracks with your death. I never should have gotten you involved in this." Her eyes shifted toward the front door. "After I heard you and Denise argue on the street, I thought you'd make for a decent distraction for the police. It never occurred to me you'd run your little investigation."

Twilight paused her escape attempts, and her scarf fell on her face. "She's the one who first told us about Denise's wrist."

"Great point, Twi." I looked at Malfina. "Why did you tell us about Denise's wrist that day I found the body? The info you gave us in Mystic Mugs inspired me to investigate."

"*Rumors*, Kinley. As a seer, I know that what people want to believe, or what they think they know, matters more than what I'd actually *see*. Matters more than the *truth*." She waved her non-wand hand through the air. "Shouldn't you know that too? Wasn't that your job? I looked into you. Public relations. Isn't that just covering up rumors with more lies?"

More nausea crept up my throat, and I found it harder to ignore than the pain. I bit the inside of my cheek. "Sometimes. Sometimes it's dispelling lies with the truth."

"Whatever. It doesn't matter. I'm ready now. This conversation was a nice distraction, though."

I heard Mark pummeling the glass in the atrium, and seconds later, a crowd of rocks hurtled into the room from down the hallway. The chunks of stone encircled us, the overhead lights catching the white and tan ribbons amongst the darker reds and grays woven into the hard surfaces.

Twilight tried to flip over and perch on her bound paws, without success. "Those. Are. Huge."

Indeed. The smallest rock rivaled my head, while the largest ranked closer to a large dog.

I pushed to my feet, but my migraine tried to knock me back to the couch. Fortunately, balance issues and I had a long history, so I managed to stay upright. "Are you going to bury us under these?"

"Yes." The word held no remorse, shame, or guilt. "You thought you were distracting me until your detective could return, didn't you? But I ensured the MBI would have quite a mess on their hands. I just needed a bit of time to extract these babies from the cliffs outside and float them through the back door."

Twilight craned her neck to catch my eye. "Kinley, you need a plan. You. Are. A. Witch. Please, DO SOME-THING! I did not just get a witch only for her to die under a mountain of stone. I did not watch *Clueless* 247 times—"

"*How many*?"

"—in the hopes of one day watching it with my own witch, only to never watch it with her."

The rocks began to rise.

No. No. No.

What could I do against powerful rocks? My magic had one use: books. So unless this house had boulder-sized books—wait.

This room was full of books. Books in the corners. A wall of books behind me.

"KINLEY!" Twilight shouted as the rocks started to sail around us, creating a gust of wind that whipped my hair around my face.

I threw my restrained arms out in front of me, sending my magic toward the corner. Tendrils of unseen magic flew from my fingertips toward the closest bookcase until they latched onto the books. With a yank, they came tumbling forward, a faint fuchsia glow around each one.

"Protect Twilight!" The books piled around her like a magical paper igloo.

I spun to the next bookcase, but Malfina had finished showing off. She sent a massive rock flying at my head. With a shriek, I dove over the back of the couch. Wasting no time, I thrust even more magic out, pulling every book off the back wall just as all the cliff pieces came rocketing toward my spot on the floor.

My much lighter books moved faster. They cocooned me in ink and paper and the smell of old books. I heaved in air as the pile of rocks crashed down, sure I'd be crushed. But the books held.

"Oh, thank frick. Or thank you, Frankenstein and Shelley," I said to the closest book to me.

The rocks lifted, only to smash back down. My book bunker shivered, but still held.

"Well, well, well," Malfina called. "The new witch can play."

I crossed my fingers she'd just give up and leave, but a harsh, grating noise had me grabbing my ears. Adrenaline had prevailed over my migraine, but that sound was stirring it up again.

"In through the nose, out through the mouth." I repeated this in my mind over and over as I inhaled and exhaled. The awful sound grew quieter as I breathed, slowly replaced by a quiet rustling.

A moment later, sand burst through the cracks between the books, diving straight for my mouth and nose. *Sand.* She'd turned the rocks to sand.

HELP! I commanded the books. *Frankenstein* tore itself apart and sealed up the cracks, but enough sand had made it through. I pulled my sweater up, but the grains tried to burrow between the threads. A little more got through with every inhale. I had to act. I needed to know where Malfina was and what she was doing.

Books! Talk to each other. Tell me what she's doing and where.

The books quivered around me before a copy of *Pride and Prejudice* burst open. The ink on the page rearranged to tell me she was directing more sand over to Twilight.

"Oh, spell no!"

I tossed a command toward Twilight's igloo, willing one of the books to seal up any holes inside. Then I asked Jane Austen, *Is there a lot more sand above me still?*

The pages nodded at me.

Okay, books, you have one job. Keep the sand away from me.

I held my fingers up.

Three. Two. One.

As one, the manuscripts and I rose. Hundreds of covers opened, flapping sand away as they whirled around me in a tornado of vicious paper.

Malfina looked over from Twilight's book burrow, where she'd just dropped a pile of sand that furiously scraped at the now-sealed cracks between covers. She raised a brow. "Impressive. But I have plenty of friends."

At least half the cliff pieces still hovered behind her. She flung three of them at me, but the flapping covers batted them away. One flew back at her head, and Malfina had to hit the floor.

I took that opportunity to go on the offensive. Raising my arms again, I called out to every last book in the house. The living room's collection was presently occupied, but this house held so many more. I doubted I'd come close to seeing them all.

Hardcovers and paperbacks crashed down the stairs and came from every direction on the main floor. I aimed them all at Malfina, intending to bury her like she'd have done to me.

But as books started to arrive, she formed her rocks into a wall, blocking the living room entryway. She left a gap big enough for a *Merriam-Webster's Collegiate Dictionary* to wiggle through. It conked her on the head.

With her concentration broken, the sand attacking me fell away, so I sent my defensive tornado of books at her. She muttered a string of curses and ducked down, calling some of her rocks into a protective dome just like I'd done with books.

"Martha, this is the worst game ever of rock, paper...sand," I said, wishing I had some scissors to defend myself. "Give it up."

"I think you mean rock, paper, wand." A yellow bolt projected from between two rocks, slicing clear through my shoulder. I screamed and collapsed to my knees.

The pain overwhelmed me, and my magic slipped from me. I held Twilight's igloo in place, but the other books fell from my grasp. Blood gushed down my arm and my back. "Sorry, Agatha," I said, opening an old Agatha Christie paperback to put pressure on the front side of the wound.

Martha would surely emerge from her cave soon. If I ran, would she chase me, leaving Twilight to live another day?

I wouldn't get far with blood exiting my body onto this copy of *Death on the Nile* faster than the actual Nile flowed, but I could try. Forcing myself to my feet, I said, "Joke's on you, Martha. Pain and I are old friends."

Her rocks started to peel away from her, so I turned to the window, preparing to jump, when instead something three times my size crashed through the glass and curtains toward me.

Glass hit my skin, but missed my eyes. I barely noticed, my attention on the beast in my living room. A roar shook Martha's rocks and rattled Twilight's little den.

The massive bear before me had a white V on its neck that I instantly recognized as belonging to a moon bear. Sundar! Somehow, even without being able to hear the commotion in my house, my neighbor had known I'd needed him.

"Oh, please," Malfina said, raising her wand.

Sundar had already leaped over a chair, his fuzzy black ears pinned back and his teeth dripping with saliva. Uncle Moonbite, indeed.

With Sundar distracting Malfina, I ignored the double dose of dizzy from both the migraine and blood loss, and submerged myself in what remained of my magic. Which is when I realized I'd almost entirely overlooked *ink*.

Which was funny, when this all started with sea sprite ink.

I tore the ink from every book in the room until I had an amorphous glob bigger than Sundar. Panting, I broke it into two halves. The first half slithered into several nets that wrestled the remaining rocks to the floor.

The other half floated over to Malfina, who'd used her wand to freeze Sundar in place, inches from making contact with her.

"Sorry, Martha. I'm all out of gold stars."

The ink collapsed on her, coating her entire body. A tendril rose from her arm and whipped her wand from her hand, throwing it out the window. More strands snapped her wrists and then her ankles together. And finally, a band of ink gagged her.

With the seer neutralized, Sundar could move again. He shifted back and rushed to my side. "Kinley...your shoulder."

"I'm okay. Maybe."

Sundar peeled back the book that I somehow still held on my shoulder. His copper eyes assessed my injury. "You are not okay. Blood's coming out both sides of the wound."

I stumbled back, and he caught me, lifting me up into his arms. "Let's find a clean spot to set you, then I'm calling for emergency transport."

"Hey!" Twilight yelled. "Let me out of here!"

Oh, right. I waved my hand, and the books fell away. Twilight vaulted off the coffee table and onto my stomach. "Kinley, oh my cauldrons. You're hurt." She looked down at the squirming seer on the rug. "Kinley, oh my cauldrons. You saved us."

A portal opened to our left, and a frazzled Ryland stepped through. His pupils blew out when he saw me, and I heard a chorus of distressed chirps from his jacket.

Keeping my eyes open grew harder, and I let my head fall onto Sundar's shoulder.

"What happened?" Ryland asked.

"Honestly? I don't know," Sundar breathed out. "I felt massive vibrations coming from the house, but I couldn't hear anything. When I came in through the open back doors, a bunch of books were attacking a solid rock wall blocking the living room, so I ran outside, shifted, and crashed through the front window. From what I gather, Malfina attacked Kinley."

I raised my eyelids enough to see that vein in Ryland's forehead pulsing again. Another portal opened, and he shouted as he stepped through it, returning seconds later with a couple of uniformed officers who moved toward

Malfina. Then he slipped his arms under me and lifted me and Twilight from Sundar. Gently, he tucked me against his chest. Just before I fell asleep, I breathed in his scent: Hints of bergamot nestled among fresh, sun-kissed laundry. Ryland smelled just like his magic felt. Cozy, safe, and warm.

Chapter Twenty-Six

"What do you think, Twi?" I gestured to the folding table I'd found in my grandmother's shed. I'd covered it with a scarlet tablecloth with twinkling stars that mirrored the night sky above us. "We've got a roaring fire, wine from Sundar's shop, and food from The Unicorn's Uncle. Owen even included a whole platter of snacks for the familiars. Too bad he had to work and couldn't join us."

Twilight came trotting across the yard from the open French doors at the back of the house. She had her new jade-green scarf with pink dragons clasped between her teeth. "Oh! I smell fish. Owen came through." She deposited the scarf at my feet. "I want to wear this for our party tonight."

I crouched to swap her fuchsia scarf for the velvety green one. "This will make your eyes pop." I tied it in an intricate knot I learned on the internet. "What do you think of my outfit?"

I stood and twirled on the toes of my boots, showing off my black pants and thick plum sweater with a scoop neck and threads of shining silver woven amidst the yarn. My typically pin-straight hair fell in curls that might just hold through the night. A spell had to exist for that. I'd even added a necklace I'd found in my grandmother's room: a little locket shaped like a book.

Twilight's pupils grew and her ears fell back. "You look amazing. I knew a makeover would pay off for you. Everything else looks great too, Kinley. You're missing one pivotal thing, though."

My eyes moved from the food and drinks to the dozen chairs around the fire, which I'd lit myself the old-fashioned human way. With wood, lighter fuel, some matches...and a little something special.

"Listen," she said.

Waves lapped against the mist-cloaked cliffs. Bats squeaked above. An owl hooted in the distance.

"What? I don't hear anything except nature."

"Exactly. Boooring. We need music. Something vibrant. Something fresh. Something that says we're glad that old witch with a 'b' didn't kill us."

I chuckled. "That sounds great, but I haven't seen any speakers around the house."

Certainly not in the living room, which Malfina and I had destroyed, only for Ryland, Sylvie, Zori, and Miguel to rebuild later that night.

By the time I'd awoken at the medical center, Twilight had told Midnight everything, so Ryland had known exactly what Malfina had done. I'd been grateful not to have to recount everything right away. The healers had already fixed my arm and restored my blood, so I hadn't needed to stay for long. The perks of magical healthcare.

I'd come home to find my witch friends fixing my living room. Everything had slid right back into place, except the copy of *Death on the Nile*, which I'd ruined with my blood. Some stains even magic couldn't erase, apparently.

The next morning, I'd had to give a detailed statement, which had also resulted in Dr. Solanum's arrest for her use of sea sprite dew. But the night I'd fought Malfina, I'd been able to come home, deliver a much-warranted hug to my semi-sentient sunflower, and slide into bed to sleep off the trauma. I suspected I had a certain detective to thank for that.

This Saturday-night oceanside bonfire was my way of thanking my friends for everything.

"We can't have a party without music!" Twilight spun in a circle. "I'll stay here. You ride your bike to the store. Get some speakers. Pink ones."

I snorted, about to tell her I wasn't leaving a cat to tend to a fire, when a voice above said, "I brought my speakers!" Azura landed and slipped a backpack off her shoulders.

A moment later, a raven thumped down on a padded chair and shifted into Shea, her legs crossed and her cane tapping the ground like a queen with her scepter. "We have to listen to Elvira's Envy."

Azura wrinkled her nose and shook her wings, a dusting of gold specks floating into the fire. "No way."

"Of course, these two can't agree on music," Zori said as she landed, Sunset popping up over her shoulder. His little nose wriggled, and he climbed out of her backpack before she even dismounted her broom. He hurried over to the snacks table to swipe a piece of bamboo.

Tansy floated through my house with her little ghost corgi, Carl, on her heels. After a shining wave to me, she informed Shea that, at the last party, they'd told Tansy she got to pick the music next. I shook my head as they bickered, deciding to stay out of it.

Dawn came bounding over next, her fuzzy yellow tail bouncing behind her. I thought she'd take out the whole food table, but Sundar darted forward to scoop his husband's familiar into his arms. Holding the massive canine like a baby, he inspected the food and started rattling off suggested pairings with the four wine options. Miguel joined him and rubbed Dawn's belly.

"Lift me so I can rub Dawn's belly too!" Twilight demanded.

Snickering, I scooped her up and took her to Dawn. "You're the weirdest feline ever." She ignored me, reaching a paw out to stroke the dog's long fur.

Sylvie touched down next to me and pulled me into a hug after she dismounted her broom. Dusk crawled out of her bag and onto my chest to wrap herself around Twilight. "Quite the spread you have, dear." Sylvie's nose twitched, but she turned away from the food and walked to the fire. "Kinley, what are you burning?"

The chatter died as all heads snapped to me. A wicked grin sprang across my face. "My wedding dress."

"And your shoes!" Twilight added, kicking her feet in the air.

"And those cursed stilettos," I said.

Everyone laughed, except Shea, who stood and waved her cane through the air. "This seems like the perfect time to tell you that Mr. Aaron Steel signed for a box of exploding glitter today at 1:13 p.m."

My jaw fell to the wet grass. "*What*?" I thought that had been a joke.

"The glitter bomb!" She made a fist and then thrust all her fingers out. "Boom. Glitter everywhere. Moon and mother, I hope he never gets it out of his ears."

Sylvie, Zori, and Miguel lost it, their cackles sailing out over the moonlit, mist-shrouded ocean. The familiars all joined in, releasing a cacophony of squeaks and howls. Azura and Sundar exchanged a look, their eyes glowing, but their lips just barely curling, like they wanted to laugh but didn't know if they should.

"Is that legal in the human world?" Azura asked.

"Yes," I said. "I think so. It wouldn't hurt him. Just...really upset him." A memory surfaced of Aaron freaking out after getting a drop of whipped cream on his *white* sweater. "*Really* upset him."

I ran forward and threw my arms around Shea, squishing Dusk and Twilight between us. After spitting out one of her red curls, I said, "Thank you. No one else has ever done anything like that for me."

She leaned her head against mine. "What are old summertime friends for if not to punish ex-fiancés?"

"Ask her what color," Twilight said.

I laughed. "Twilight wants to know what color glitter you ordered."

Shea pulled away to look at her. "Pink, of course."

Twilight pumped a paw into the air. "Yes!"

Thirty minutes passed as everyone ate and mingled. I surveyed the area to make sure everyone was having a good time. Sylvie brought me a plate of fries and gave me a knowing look. "He'll be here."

"What? Who?"

"I see you looking around every two seconds, Kinley."

Of course, Ryland chose that moment to open a portal eight feet away and step through with his bright-purple sneakers. A big plastic container sat in his hands, a tiny dragon perched on top. "Sorry I'm late. The decorating took longer than I thought."

A flutter in my abdomen, as if Midnight had flapped his little wings in my stomach, had me turning my gaze to the fire, where my marshmallow of a dress roasted like a, well, marshmallow. All my hopes for a life I'd realized I'd never wanted...now reduced to embers.

So what did I want?

I flicked my eyes to the food table. Ryland had slipped out of his jacket, revealing a charcoal sweater that fit him *very* well. He was carefully setting out some of the most beautiful cupcakes I'd ever seen. Not only were they huge—just how I liked my desserts—the piles of icing on top unfurled into delicate book pages so that each cupcake looked like a book in motion, its pages caught in a breeze. Well, I guess I wanted a cupcake. Maybe that was all I needed to know for now.

"Holy hexes. Kinley, get over here!" Twilight waved me over with her tail. "Does he expect you to *eat* these? They belong in a museum!"

Midnight puffed his chest up proudly on Ryland's shoulder as the compliments poured in. I stepped up to the opposite side of the table from him and set my fries down.

"Ry, these are..." I cleared my throat. "These are beautiful."

The gold specks in his eyes grew brighter. "Thanks, Kinley. Consider these your official welcome to Sea Sprite...no tackling through a portal involved."

My lips quirked. "You can't take back the tackle welcome—you'll never live that down—but I'm honored to have these as a follow up. Though..." I bit my lip.

"What?"

"I'm not sure I can actually eat one. They're too pretty!"

With a devilish smirk, he swiped a finger through one and smeared the icing on my cheek.

I gaped at him, unsure if I should throw a fry or arrest him for ruining good art, but then an ethereal hum rose above the Fleetwood Mac playlist our '70s ghost had ultimately chosen.

"They're back," Sylvie said, voice thick with awe.

Azura flew over and grabbed my arm, pulling me toward the ocean. A moment later, a line of six-inch sea sprites rose above the cliffs. A dozen had graced us with their presence during morning yoga, but tonight we had at least twice that number.

Their dusty-purple glow seemed to disappear around their wings, fading into the darkness as they emerged from the mist and flew a few feet over the lawn. The temperature dropped, ice forming on the grass beneath them. I'd thought them beautiful and ethereal in the morning light, but lit only by the moon and the fire, I forgot to breathe. My magic stirred under my skin, recognizing the gravity of the moment.

The same sprite who'd led the choreographed retreat on Tuesday initiated a new dance. It started off soft before transitioning to a layered rush of wings and bodies that mimicked the furious waves of a storm.

Just when the sprites' movements grew so frantic I was sure they couldn't go on, the dance broke into something mournful yet grateful. They flew in figure eights, touching their palms to each other's as they passed. Then they slowed, forming a straight line, and bowing, all their eyes on me.

A bit of salt hit my tongue, and I realized I'd shed a tear. The sprites had told us their story. What they'd felt being targeted by poachers, and their relief at having one of their enemies exposed. But there'd be more. Someone would always come for them.

I bowed back, and the sprites broke off, one from each end, until only the sprite in the middle remained. She twiddled her fingers and dove down the cliffs.

Azura squeezed my arm before walking away. The noise picked up behind me, but I just watched the mist for a minute, not minding how chilly it felt this far from the fire. The magical world had embraced me, and I'd seen so many wondrous things, but this world held its own sets of challenges. Its own greedy, nasty people.

Over the dark cliffs, the last sea sprite rose again. She flew directly to me, held my gaze for a moment, and in a voice like an echo off the ocean, whispered, "She lives."

A pang for something I'd never had threatened to collapse my chest cavity. I reached for my sternum, just to make sure it still existed.

A tear dripped from the sprite's eye as many more slipped from my own.

She departed again, and I heaved in a breath, trying to stabilize myself. A brush of warmth like a basket of fresh linens told me Ryland had arrived at my side. His solid presence helped steady me, as did Midnight's concerned meep.

I smiled when I realized he held Twilight under one arm too. My familiar wriggled around until she could crawl onto my shoulder and rub her face in my neck.

"What did she tell you, Kinley?" Ryland asked.

After a quick look behind me to confirm no one could hear, I looked up at his earnest expression. "'She lives.'"

"Who lives?"

I tugged my sleeves farther over my hands. "The sprite didn't say, but I could *feel* it, Ry. I think she meant my mother."

Ryland ran a hand over the back of his head before nodding. "Then we'll find her." He locked eyes with me. "If you want."

I shook my head. "They looked already. For years."

He reached down and took my palm in his fingers, squeezing it gently before releasing it. "They didn't have the sea sprites' favor. And they didn't have *you*. Kinley, the magic you did against Martha Malfina the other night...it went beyond impressive. With your bibliomancy and my investigation skills, we might be able to do this." Midnight chirped and beat his wings.

I bit the inside of my cheek, and Twilight put her head on top of mine. "Kinley, I can feel you're scared," she said. "What if we can't find her? What if we do and it turns out she just didn't want you?" My gut swirled. She'd read me like Page read souls. I was terrified. "But what if she *needs* us, Kinley?"

Hexes. Sylvie had said she thought my parents meant to return to Sea Sprite, but couldn't. So if my mother still lived three decades later but couldn't return, maybe she did need us. I took a steadying breath.

Ryland ran a finger over his bottom lip. "I have an idea, if you're open to it."

Grabbing his arm, I spun us around. "Tell me your idea. But I'm eating a cupcake or four first."

THE END

Kinley, Twilight, and pals will return in *Spell to Pay*, coming soon!

Stay up to date on new releases by signing up for Elle's newsletter at https://elleburkeauthor.com/

Thank you!

Thank you for reading *What the Spell?* I hope you enjoyed the wondrous world on Sea Sprite Isle as much as I enjoyed writing it. Can I ask you a favor? If you have a few minutes, can you leave a review on Amazon or Goodreads? I would really appreciate it. Reviews mean everything to authors.

For the scoop on upcoming books, insider info, and more fun content, join **Elle's Facebook reader group** at https://www.facebook.com/groups/ellewrenburke.

Follow me on:
Instagram @ellewrenburke.author
Facebook @ellewrenburke

About the Author

Elle is just a pale gal hiding from the sun in one of the sunniest states in the US. She prioritizes humor in her own life and the books she writes. On any given day, you'll find her snuggling a dog, a pillow, or a good book—maybe all three—while she recovers from exerting way more energy than her disabilities authorized. Elle lives with Hypermobile Ehlers-Danlos Syndrome, a connective tissue disease, fibromyalgia, and migraines. She enjoys puzzles, baking, and board games.

Learn more about Elle and stay up to date on new books at
https://elleburkeauthor.com/
Join Elle's Facebook reader group at
https://www.facebook.com/groups/ellewrenburke.
Follow me on:
Instagram @ellewrenburke.author
Facebook @ellewrenburke

Also By Elle Wren Burke

Chatty Cat Mysteries
Purrs & Poison
Meows & Murder
Felines & Felonies

Vampire Pet Boutique Mysteries
A Fang to Remember
The Tell-Fang Heart
A Midsummer Fang's Dream
Best Fangs Forever

Prickly Pear Psychic Mysteries
Mediums & Murder
Tea & Talismans
Canines & Cacti
Mascara & Mayhem
Peril & Paperbacks